T0105784

ЯƎVƎЯ2Ǝ
FORWARD

A Novel

YVONNE
DIDWAY

WestBow
PRESS
A DIVISION OF THOMAS NELSON

Copyright © 2012 Yvonne Didway.

All rights reserved. No part of this book may be used or reproduced by any means, graphic, electronic, or mechanical, including photocopying, recording, taping or by any information storage retrieval system without the written permission of the publisher except in the case of brief quotations embodied in critical articles and reviews.

WestBow Press books may be ordered through booksellers or by contacting:

WestBow Press
A Division of Thomas Nelson
1663 Liberty Drive
Bloomington, IN 47403
www.westbowpress.com
1-(866) 928-1240

Because of the dynamic nature of the Internet, any web addresses or links contained in this book may have changed since publication and may no longer be valid. The views expressed in this work are solely those of the author and do not necessarily reflect the views of the publisher, and the publisher hereby disclaims any responsibility for them.

Any people depicted in stock imagery provided by Thinkstock are models, and such images are being used for illustrative purposes only.

Certain stock imagery © Thinkstock.

ISBN: 978-1-4497-3149-6 (sc)
ISBN: 978-1-4497-3150-2 (e)
Library of Congress Control Number: 2011960446

Printed in the United States of America

WestBow Press rev. date: 1/27/2012

Contents

To my sister Megan, without you this book
would still be hidden in my journal.
Oh, and I won the bet. ;)

Preface

Okay, so here's the thing, I starting writing this book when I was 13. It's been done for a little over four years now; I've just been too insecure to let anyone read it. So here it is. Finally. I am opening up a piece of me to you. I hope you enjoy what you read, but I also hope you look beyond the words and pages and let it speak to you.

This book has a lot of reflections of my life, however, it is not a biography, or in any way a story about me. An author writes from what they know, and at the time, this was all I knew, and could come up with through my imagination.

"Love from the center of who you are."★

Von <3

P.S. here are a couple of my favorite verses that I think you should check out. :)

Isaiah 54:10 (msg)

★Romans 12: 9–10a (msg)

Acknowledgements

First off, I want to thank my best friend; He has been there with me every step of the way. Encouraging me, helping me, and simply loving me for me. He has been my rock, my shelter, my hope, my peace, and my calm-down-every-thing-is-going-to-be-fine. Thanks God, you are pretty great!

Secondly, I want to thank my family, my brothers, Nate, Matt and Andy, and their wives Megan, Emily and Keri for being my biggest fans and pushing me to keep on pursuing my dream. A big thanks to my Aunt Carolyn, for being my first professional editor; and for all of her help extending my knowledge on the art of writing. Megan, thank you for all of those long nights of giggling and working on the book, for telling me to keep extending my work, to keep pushing the limits of my creativity, and for telling me when something was lame. You are amazing and a huge part of why this dream is finally in book form. My daddy (the king on the castle) for keeping me grounded and thinking with a clear head, and my mom. Mom, you have been so wonderful through this whole process. I honestly don't know what I would do without you. And to my grandparents, for being a huge part in making my dream of publishing a book come true. Thank you for being the greatest business partners and grandparents any girl could ask for. I love you!

And lastly, of course, a shout out to all my friends, Drexel, Mo-Town, HKY, SRPC, all my Camp Wo-Jo buddies, I-heart and everyone and anyone I didn't mention. I feel like I already have a fan group. You guys are great and I love each and every one of you so much!

I love you all so much, thanks for all the encouragement. I couldn't have done it without all of you.

Introduction

"I began to realize it on the Hill. The Hill opened my eyes to another world. My world. It is crazy how one simple hill can change a life. My life."

-Yvonne Didway
Journal entry

Prologue

Dear mommy,

I learned that the smallest things can change lives, like a smile from a stranger, or three simple words "I love you". I have learned to let things go, to cherish the great moments and to forget the ugly ones. I have learned that if it wasn't for what happened and the pressure it put on me to grow up in some areas, I would still be the same sad, quiet Blair. The Blair that never talked, never looked up as someone passed by and the Blair that was terrified of acceptance and failure.

I'm sitting at my same spot on the hill; you would love this place mom. The hill is forgotten and overgrown, the damp ground is soaking into my jeans and the sky is clear blue like after a hard rain. I can just see you sitting here with me, with your sketchpad, doodling away; I miss simply sitting next to you. It's all the same every time I come, but that makes it even more beautiful to me. It's the only place I feel steady, that's not always changing on me.

I'm thinking about the old me and why the heck was I like that? I still don't know, and I'm not sure I'll ever "really" know. Could it have something to do with you not being here mom, and that I was scared of facing the people and their sympathy? It's starting to become clear to me, when I heard the fake understanding in the voices, it just made it seem even more real, and I couldn't handle that. I couldn't handle you being gone.

-Your little bumble bee<3

Chapter 1

Trapped

Another *day went by as she sat in her room, refusing to come out; trapped in a sea of lies, waiting. Waiting for what? She longs to be rescued, but is haunted by the repressive fear of being torn apart. As she sat for what seemed like an eternity, she could hear the blood curdling screams of the angry mob as the pounding in her head reciprocated the rhythmic beating of fists on the door. Her only recurring thought was, "It's all my fault! How can I* **stop** *this? How can I stop this?" Her family says they still love her, but how could they after what she has done? In a state of confusion she struggles with the decision to open the door and let the angry mob tear her apart, or does she stay . . . stay locked up in the dungeon she thought she knew as her bedroom. She can hear the mob trying to beat down the door. The splintering wood is flying everywhere! She tries to run, but there's nowhere to go! With a loud crash, the door falls to pieces . . .*

I sit up straight on my daybed, breathing hard, pushing my sheets down to my ankles. It's still dark outside; the air is tranquil, hot and sticky. I run my fingers through my tangled hair and try to slow my breathing. I don't understand why this dream keeps coming back every night the same dream just different variations. I lean back resting against my headboard; my alarm clock says its five twenty one. Too early, to get up on a Saturday, but there's no way I'll be able to fall back to sleep, chills run up my spine as I remember the dream. I roll out of bed and decide not to take a shower *I just want to be a bum today, well at least till dad gets up.* I went over to my closed door and turn the knob hoping dad fixed the squeaky hinges. *Ah he did,* I smiled. I tiptoed to his room across from mine and paused to peak through the slightly opened door. I giggled; he was out like a light, snoring and everything. He claims he doesn't snore but one day I'm going to record him and win this debate. I shut his door as quietly as I can and start to go down stairs.

Before my descent, my reflection in the hall mirror stops me mid step. I stand there for a while not knowing why I stopped. I look at the small girl staring back at me. I look down not willing to face myself. I've always felt awkward staring at myself in the mirror, it just doesn't seem natural. Slowly I pull my head up and make myself look at the bummy mess that I am. I take in the scar on the left side of my forehead, my dark, thick eyelashes, the light freckles on my nose and my bright pink lips, the lower slightly fuller than the top. Many women have told me that they would kill to have lashes like mine. I really don't get it, they're just eyelashes. I don't think that they match the rest of my face. I just think that they stand out compared to my pale features.

I look deep into my green eyes, I get them from my dad, just to find the sparkle has gone and has yet to come back. I'm really not sure if it ever will. I don't want to look any longer, but something inside me won't let me pull away. My soft cheeks that can easily become bright red are marked with sleep lines from my pillowcase. My friend Connor is always teasing me about how much I blush. My messy blonde hair is falling out of the bun I tied it in before bed. The pink highlights I added over the summer just to drive my best friend crazy, are starting to fade. I step away from the mirror laughing at the memory of Jen's face when she saw my hair for the first time. She cares more than I do about how *I* look. I was seriously surprised that my dad loved it, I'm still not sure if I should be entirely freaked out or bummed that he didn't go berserk.

I made my way down the stairs trying to avoid the squeaky parts and tripping over my own feet. I went into the kitchen grabbed a box of *honey nut cheerios* and plopped down on the couch. Stuffed a handful of cereal in my mouth and then turned on the TV. I watched Saturday morning cartoons, something I haven't done in ages, until I heard my dad come down the stairs, not missing a single squeaky step.

"Why are you up so early, doll?" my dad said as he approached the couch.

"I donno, had a weird dream." I said stuffing another handful of cereal in my mouth, so I wouldn't have to answer any more questions. Dad gave me a suspicious look with his deep green eyes.

"Don't worry dad; it was just a random dream." I attempted to say with my mouth full.

"Well . . . okay." He gave me one last concerned look, before he walked to the kitchen to grab some breakfast.

"Hey dad?" I yell hoping he can hear me in the kitchen.

"Yes doll?" he yells back.

"I think I'm going to go for a run around the block, I'll be back in a little."

"Okay, be careful, watch out for crazy drivers." I laugh and drag myself upstairs to change out of my sweats and oversized hoodie, I'm pretty sure I stole it from one of my brothers. Whatever.

★   ★   ★

Dear mommy,

Running to me is poetry, the rhythm of my feet hitting the pavement, the slow, deep breaths in through my nose out through my mouth, the ache in my chest; it all flows together and creates a luring comfort. People find comfort in rhythm, the slow steady beat of a song, the constant tick of a clock, the lulling pace of a heart beat. Rhythm is steady, never changing, unless someone comes in and hits pause on your CD player, or the batteries in your kitchen clock run out. I find comfort in the pace when I run, although it feels like I'm dying afterwards from an asthma attack, it still puts me at ease. I remember when you would come through the door after you went for a run; you looked like you were dying, ha-ha. I must get that from you.

Did I get this comfort of running from you? When I run I focus on the pace, the rhythm, instead of what all is going on in this crazy world. I don't think about the bills daddy forgot to pay, and about what we're going to have for dinner. I forget about my crazy friends and all their petty drama, but mostly I forget about me. I forget about you. I stop feeling sorry for myself and everything that's happened and happening. I just simply run.

-Your little humble bee. <3

Chapter 2

Beautiful

When I roll out of bed the next morning, a sudden queasy feeling starts up in my stomach when the thought comes to me,

I start school tomorrow . . .

I lug myself to the bathroom and start my shower, hoping the steam will clear my head. My heart is heavy, knowing that the summer has ended and the sun will soon start fading, the trees will grow brown and the sky grey. School will consume my life again and dad will start fixing up the house, just like he does every fall, (you would think he would in the spring like everyone else?). I like our little house, it's very bachelor pad-ish. Well, the outside isn't because I made him paint it pastel yellow, and he keeps flowers in the little garden nice and neat and trims the bushes, but the inside is a whole new story. When you first walk in, to your right is our little living room, where dad watches all the football and basketball games, and my best friends and I spend every Friday night watching movies and doing whatever it is that we do, we're a very random bunch. When we moved in, dad said that three things were a must, our huge tan leather couch that we have had since before I was born, a big screen TV and the *Gladiator* poster. The kitchen consists of paper plates; take out, steak and organic fruit. A typical dad and daughter fridge, if you ask me.

I went downstairs after I got dressed to have breakfast with daddy. The day was beautiful, hot sunny skies, sidewalks so hot it burns your feet if you try and walk barefooted. It was my kind of day. After breakfast we rushed off to church noticing the time; we're late.

Of course, I seriously doubt we've ever been on time.

Dad and I spend a lazy Sunday at the beach, after we get back from church, people watching and building a sand castle. I know I'm probably a little old for sand castles since I'm sixteen and all but that's just kind of our thing. Sappy? Yes, but I love it.

"It seems to me we can never give up longing and wishing while we are thoroughly alive. There are certain things we feel to be beautiful and good, and we must hunger after them."
-George Eliot

Dear mommy,

I wonder if my love for the sun is something I found for myself or is this something else I got from you? Everything I do I wonder what I will never know, what I get from you by simply having the same genes or what I picked up as a little kid. Even though it's hard to face the reality that I will never know the answers to these questions I still ask them knowing that it's beautiful because without this beauty of wonder I don't know how I would handle you being gone . . .

You taught me to find the beauty in everything, I think I'm finally grasping what you meant by that, and understanding how to find it. There's this cute little grandma and gramps sitting together under an umbrella, a little ways away from where I'm sitting. They're adorable mom; you would truly be inspired by them. They're holding hands, watching, what I presume, their grandkids playing in the waves. When I see old people in love it make me smile, but there's always that subtle pain for dad. I question sometimes how he can even say the word 'love' without breaking down . . . I know this couple must be true love, their wrinkles are almost matching, showing many years together. I'm sure they went through many tiffs and hard times, but yet even a stranger like me sees the glisten in their eyes as they smile at each other. Is this one of those moments you were talking about? Things like when a cut is healing, it amazes me how our bodies just up and start to rebuild. It's so ugly, but there's so much beauty in it. Or when your heart is broken and feels like you can't move on, but yet you do . . . one word: Beautiful.

Your little bumble bee <3

★　　★　　★

The next morning, Monday, I woke up from one of those terrible dreams again; I just wish they would go away. I walked down the dark blue carpeted stairs (not very gracefully might I add), and Dad was rinsing off a skillet in our blue sink. "Good morning Daddy."

"Morning' doll!" *He is way too chipper for the morning.* "You ready for your first day of tenth grade?"

"Way to start the day: being reminded of going back to school. "He laughed at me and sat down a plate of eggs and bacon in the shape of a smiley face on the worn table. "Come and eat." I smiled and sat down and grabbed a fork.

"hey um, do you think we could leave a little early, Jen told me to meet her at the picnic tables before school to walk in together. She has this weird phobia of walking in alone, like something's going to be in her nose or teeth or that she'll trip over something, so she wants me to be there to make sure those things don't happen."

He laughed and nodded his head, and mumbled something about Jen. No one really knows what's going on in her head; she's really great, but a bit crazy.

When I finished my breakfast I went upstairs to start the water for my shower. I brushed my teeth, straight from four painful and annoying years of braces and pulled my long dark blonde hair out if the knot it was in from sleeping with it in a hair tie.

I let the pelting hot water massage the knots out of my back and neck and the steam clear my head. After I was done with everything that had to do with a shower, I reached out and grabbed a towel and stepped out in the process slipping on a wadded up towel, thankfully this time I caught myself on the towel rack, I have quite a few bruises from falling on this stupid floor. After gathering myself and steadying my balance, I brushed out my wet hair and blow dried it slightly, so it wasn't a soppy mess; I twisted it back into a low bun, and let it dry the rest of the way on its own. I put on a little eye shadow ignoring the mascara, there's no way I'm going to make my eyelashes even more dramatic, the only reason for even putting eye shadow on is to avoid the lecture from Jen. I walked into my room; went to my walk-in closet to see what Jen had me wearing for the first day of school. I ignored the prearranged outfits she picked out (yeah I guess you could say she's a little obsessive) for me and picked out my own thing; a blue jean mini skirt with my purple high top converses, and a white V neck tee. I threw my outfit on and ran down stairs and rushed my dad to leave.

Chapter 3

Typical

I walked up to the courtyard of my old, musty, but beautiful private school, pulling my hair out of the bun and let it fall into place; it was sunny with a subtle cool breeze. I could already see the different cliques forming: Cheerleaders in their new short pleated maroon and gold skirts gossiping by the fountain; Goths in their baggy black pants with chains dragging on the ground, smoked by the huge tree (talk about a fire hazard), and the skaters attempting to do, whatever they do on that death board. Knowing me, if I ever tried to step on one of those things I would probably fall and break something and die. I cringe at the vision of me dying, it looks painful, and I don't do very well with pain. I snap out of my morbid thoughts and walk around the corner of the building to where Jen told me to meet her. There aren't many people back behind the building where the stone picnic tables are, as I approached to sit on top of one. Jen has dark brown eyes, almost black, that matched her shoulder length dark hair that is always perfect; she never has a hair out of place. She was wearing a semi-short preppy schoolgirl plaid skirt with a white polo and red flats and layered different necklaces. She could wear a sack and still look good, and I have no idea how she does it. Jenna says, quote, "The best part of this school is that we can basically wear whatever we want." End quote. For a private school I have to agree. That's a typical Jenna statement, she talks a lot about clothes and make up and a whole lot of other stuff that I don't understand. Despite all her crazy, she's one of the sweetest persons you'll ever meet. My other best friend, Conner is a shy, baby-faced blonde; he's tall and wears simple clothes, mostly ironic tees, he thinks they are hilarious.

"Hey!" Jenna squealed and gave me a squeeze around my shoulders.

"Hey" I said smiling. I looked around her for Connor.

"What's up with you?"

"Good"

"What?" she said, giving me a confused look.

"Wait; what did you just say?"

"I said what's up, and then you said 'good'?"

"Oh, sorry, I wasn't paying attention."

"You okay? You look lost."

"Yeah, I'm fine; where's Connor?"

"Umm, I don't know, he must not be here yet."

"Oh okay, I just thought he was coming with you."

"Look!" Jen said as we walked through the door. She tapped me on my shoulder so fast and hard I thought I was going to have a hole in my clavicle! There he stood, leaning over, taking a long drink from the water fountain.

"This deserves a moment of silence." Jen said while googahhing over Logan. I laughed to myself at her as she stood there, looking like a loon drooling over the "oh-so-hot" Logan.

Jen has had a crush on him since middle school, so of course he's off limits, but I do have to admit he is *very* attractive. He's the typical California boy: tall, blond, tanned and handsome. He has the girlfriend—Mandy—that looked like she just stepped off the runway or out of hell, whichever one you prefer to say, who all the girls hated. They have been an on and off again couple for like a zillion years. Of course he's the captain of the football team and *she* thinks she runs the school. They're the kind of couple that you would see in a cheesy Disney movie. You know, the hottie that the main girl wanted, but the evil girlfriend gets in the way, but it all turns out okay because the girl realizes she's not in love with the hottie, but is in love with her guy best friend. In other words: crap.

"I hate her." I said jokingly, but half-way serious.

"He is so fine." Jen added.

"Mhm, have you gotten your schedule yet?"

"Yup!" she is way too alive for it to be morning.

"Walk with me to get mine."

"Okay," she smiled. "So, like you know that guy I was talking to . . ." This is when I lose focus. With Jen all you have to do is nod every once in a while and say uh huh, and she totally thinks you're paying attention.

"Okay! Girl, you look so cute!" she interrupted herself, "Where did you get that skirt?" she asked with an open mouthed wink.

I laughed at her. "I don't remember things like that, probably a thrift store or something." she looked mortified

"-uh, B-"

"Hold the lecture." I teased.

She laughed at my comment, "okay, okay, but I do have to admit those shoes are very cute with that outfit." She looked like she just committed a crime. Her dark eyes brightened, "I am so proud!" she hugged me again.

Jen was the one that kept me *in style*; if it were up to me I would just wear jeans and a tee to school. But she won't let me do that, she says that if I'm going to wear jeans they have to fit, and not be from last year, or five years ago in my case.

When she first met me in ninth grade, she was so excited to have a 'plain' confused girl to turn in to her little project, to what you would call 'fashionable'. I wanted to be *in style,* I mean I am a girl, but just never knew how. My dad's best friend, Uncle Joe, his wife Sue, tried (the operative word being tried) to help me keep up with clothing, but I was a lost cause. She wanted me to wear pink and ruffles, and I refused.

Jen took me shopping and taught me how to do my hair. She showed me that by parting it on the right side it would cover my scar on the left side of my forehead, obtained by chasing my brother Rob outside, when he climbed a tree, I followed and he playfully pushed me into a branch that stabbed me in the forehead. Rough life, I know.

Jen taught me the right amount of make up to put on, and how to organize my closet. I was exhausted when the day was over, but I finally understood (somewhat) the world of being a girl, *at least a little better.*

At the end of this summer I caught her in my closet organizing and pinning 'post it's' that said when and where to wear them, onto every outfit! Got to love Jen.

Chapter 4

Noob

"Okay class, listen up," my homeroom teacher barked out. She was a sight. I thought I was bad when it came to dressing, but she—well, let's just say it's mine and Jen's mission, before we graduate, to bring her in to the new millennium. Yeah, it's bad enough for me to notice. Last year's Amish skirts and over sized sweaters have been outdone by the muumuu this morning. The seats squeaked as students settled in. I grabbed my phone out of my back pocket to text Connor to see if his flight had been delayed last night. Mrs. Web's (what kind of name is that in the first place?) Teacher like boom interrupted my concerned thoughts with an announcement

"We have three new students this year, Tessa Young, Jacob Hoyle," she pointed to the back of the room as the new bees tried to keep it cool, "oh it looks like Joshua Bates is late. Now every—"

"What!" I spouted.

"Excuse me, Miss Chance, is there a problem?"

"Uh, no, I uh just thought of something . . . sorry." I slumped lower into my desk. But really I was startled by the thought of the Joshua Bates I knew in Florida. I was born in Florida and lived there for my elementary and middle school years. I moved the summer after eighth grade. Josh was one of the "popular" kids, and I sure enough wasn't.

There was a knock on the door, I jumped.

"What was all of that about?" Jen asked beside me.

"Uh, don't worry about it, I'll tell you later." The knock triggered a flashback to the hysterical dreams I've been having lately, and if they don't stop soon my dad's going to catch on.

"Oh, well I need some volunteers to show Tessa and Jacob around campus. Anyone?" my teacher interrupted my thoughts again. Some lanky freckled face kid in the back raised his hand for the chick. Johnny from last year's history raised his for Jacob.

"Blair Chance you almost have the exact same schedule as Joshua, so you'll be showing him around when he gets here." she said in a sarcastic tone.

"Are you serious?"

"Yes" the teacher said quickly. Obviously moving down her check list and totally oblivious to my negative outburst. *Just my luck* . . . I leaned over to Jen and whispered, "What's Mrs. Web's problem? Her girdle too tight?"

"No way if anything, that muumuu could fit Santa Claus, she could go without wearing one and there still would be room in that thing, it's huge!" I covered my face before Mrs. Webs could see that I was laughing.

"Oh here he is," she announced obviously not seeing us laughing. An assortment of "heys" and "hi's," but more groans than anything came from the class. People whispering to each other about who knows what and me, not laughing anymore, in horror because it **was** the Joshua Bates I knew . . .

For the rest of first period, I sat nervously thinking about what I was going to say to Joshua. I wasn't nervous about him **not** remembering me; I was scared he **would** remember me.

★   ★   ★

It all started in sixth grade, the first year of middle school. Sixth grade was great, if you carried a *Coach* (those were the shiz back then) and were *popular*. I was **not**. I was just Blair Chance, small quiet and shy. I sat by the trash cans at lunch. The popular kids always had a seat open, but you had to be 'chosen' to sit with them; it was so elementary school if you ask me; but of course, nobody did. Then there were the kids that didn't seem to care what you thought about them, they just had fun. I didn't fit in to either one of those categories, so I just made myself invisible.

Dear mommy,

Looking back on it now, I shouldn't have been so insecure; daddy had the money for me to have all the 'cool' stuff that the popular kids had, but I didn't have the social skills and the looks or the attitude to be one. As shallow as it all is, back then I really wanted to be one—or at least to stand out more than I did. You warned me about how hard these years were going to be. You said that many of your middle school students expressed heartache, confusion and especially insecurity in their art work. Many times, you theorized, sixth grade turns out to be one of the hardest years socially, mentally, emotionally and physically. You had encouraged me to think of it as a year to start over; being done with elementary school, primary colors and moving from long division in to pre-algebra. I didn't get it at the time; that you weren't going to be with me during my sixth grade year. I thought you would be there alongside me every awkward step of the way. I know now that you were preparing me to take that first awkward step alone. I was so confused and lost that I just didn't step up at all, much less to your challenge when I should have.

Your little bumble bee <3

To add to my sixth grade woes; I had a bottom locker because I was (and always will be) short, and the kid above me just loved to get his stuff out at the same time, so he literally stood over me. Talk about awkward . . . Because I was short, skinny and lanky with glasses and braces, no guys looked at me, and the preppy girls didn't ask me to sleepovers. Zilch. Nadda. Nothing.

I only had one friend, Ricky. Ricky and I grew up with each other, our moms were practically sisters. We really didn't become close friends, however, until fifth grade when my mom passed away with cancer. He and his mom would come over every night to cook dinner for my dad and me and my three older brothers. We grew very close during that couple of months. He would sit beside me at lunch and make me eat something; if it weren't for him, who knows? I would probably have been hospitalized for malnutrition. He was my best friend.

Sixth grade passed and no one talked to us. We went through our days alongside everyone else, but not really with anyone else.

Seventh grade came, and it was more of the same, except Ricky was growing in to his extremely long legs and becoming quite the "hottie." Girls started talking to him and trying to use me to get to him. I finally got tired of my 'friends' using me and Ricky eating it all up, so I told him it had to stop, he tried, but fell for the fluttering eyelashes again shortly therafter. Ricky and I were no more.

Finally, after a long and lonely summer, eighth grade came. I was starting to fill out, but was still a tooth pick. My eighth grade year was going great; I started hanging out with some girls from the Beta Club and even started talking to a boy named Tim. But one day in January, Thursday the twenty-first to be exact, it all disappeared . . .

I was changing in to my normal clothes after PE when the cheerleaders came running in screaming "there's a fire!" They picked me up before I had a chance to put on my top and carried me out. Come to find out, no fire, the joke was on me. I stood there in my bra and jean shorts. Frozen. I didn't know what to do! They had carried me in to the gym where the boy's basketball team was practicing. I started to cry and hid, mortified, in the janitor's closet until everyone had gone home. As I sat beside mop buckets, under a shelf of Clorox and other strong smelling cleaners, I could hear students in the hall way talking about "double A" and the "fire drill." I wanted to cry again, but knew that if someone opened that door, my pride could not take another hit. Somehow I made it out of there and at home

I faked being sick until the weekend. For the rest of my eighth grade year I was teased about the unplanned fire drill. People I didn't even know called me *double A*, which isn't true. I was almost a full B!

Chapter 5

Liar

As I sat day dreaming about my unfortunate past, I was startled to reality by a deep voice.

"Um, are you Blair Chance?" I jumped!

"What the-!"

"Sorry I didn't mean to scare you."

"Uh, it's okay . . ." I said trying to hide my face with my long hair. He had changed a little, but of course, just my luck, he was still gorgeous. He wore black converses with lyrics to songs written all over them, I tried to peak through my hair to read them, but no luck, however, I did notice his jeans, skinny to be exact. I slowly looked up through my hair, still trying to hide my face. His navy blue Hurley t-shirt was tighter than most guys should wear them, but on him it worked, just for the simple fact that he was hot. He was a lot taller, and his normally shaggy "Beiber hair" was now a short foux-hawk. You can actually see his eyes . . . *Wow* . . . deep, crystal blue, the very same eyes that I fell for four years ago. The very same ones that made me melt into an ocean of crystal when he glanced my way and we accidently made awkward eye contact. *Ahh those eyes . . .*

"I'm Josh," he said with curiosity in his voice.

Yes you are.

"Oh hi," I said awkwardly looking away. "I'm, uh . . ."
oh gosh . . . what do I say?

"Blair," Jen said coolly behind me. "Her name is Blair,
and I'm Jen," I blushed and used my hair to hide it

"I'm Josh. It's very nice to meet you both," he said
with a wink. Jen giggled. *Yes this was definitely the same
arrogant, flirty Josh I knew and couldn't stand, but yet was so in
love with . . .* I thought while rolling my eyes.

"I think Blair is supposed to be my tour guide for the
day?" He said flashing me a perfect smile.

"Uh huh." I said trying to sound enthusiastic. It was
quiet for way to long, until Jen finally broke the silence.

"We should get going before the bell rings." She gave
me a look that said *go you duffice! He's hot!* The first bell
rang and I hopped up, straightened my skirt, and then led
the way to the crowded hall.

"So, where is your next class?" I choked out trying not
to look at his crystal clear, blue eyes.

"Um, history—I think." he said looking confused at
his schedule.

"Oh okay, it's this way." I directed him to the far end
of the hall.

"Sweet Thanks."

"Yeah" I said not really agreeing with the "sweet"
part of that sentence. I felt watched, like he was trying to
catch a glance of me every so often. I kept my head down
looking at the floor and the top edge of my books that I
was squeezing very tightly in my arms.

"You don't talk much do you?"

I laughed, remembering him saying that almost word for word at my locker so many years ago . . .

"My dad always taught me to not talk to strangers." He grinned and looked at me.

"Are you sure we are strangers?" I *froze. Crap he does recognize me* . . . "Because you look *really* familiar."

I tripped over my own feet, catching myself before he could notice. *He does remember me. Do I lie or tell the truth?*

"Uh, no . . . not that I know of," I said looking away. *I'm an awful liar . . .*

"You sure?"

I laughed, trying to play it off, "unless you saw me in the grocery store or something, but I'm pretty sure I've never seen you before." he paused and chuckled. "You know what it is? Yeah, there was this girl I knew back home that you remind me of."

"Oh." That was all I could get out, hoping it wasn't 'me' he was talking about. *Which duh Blair, of course it was 'you' who else would it be?*

"She was kind of the dorky type, Cute though, but-"

Yep, definitely me . . . wait did he say cute? yep definitely me. I laughed at myself.

"Uh, thanks?" I said interrupting, not wanting to hear the rest of his sentence. *I thought my dorky days were over? Ok B, recap—Did he say she was a cute dork, or I was a cute dork? And the male gender says girls were confusing!*

"Oh dang! Sorry, that came out way wrong, I meant **she** was kind of dorky, not you . . ." he looked down, embarrassed.

"It's okay, I really am a dork." I gave him a subtle reassuring smile.

"Aw, well I don't believe you. I thought she was cute, but she was painfully shy and only talked to this one kid . . . uh . . ."

"Ricky." I said not intending my thoughts to be heard.

"Yeah" he looked at me and smiled, before his expression changed. "Wait . . . how did you know his name?"

"Uh . . . That kid we just passed his name is Ricky . . ." I lied. *OH geese . . .*

"Oh." he said suspiciously.

"Here we are room 201." I said trying to change the subject before I opened my big mouth again.

B don't even let yourself think about back then, just let it go, it's the past, just ignore it.

"Thanks." he said smiled and walked to the back of the class.

"Uh huh . . ." I'm supposed to sit next to Connor since we found out we had the same history class. But when I walked in he wasn't there. I look at the clock; he should have been here an hour ago. I don't get it, what's going on with him. And where is he?

Why hasn't he texted me back?

I was really hoping he was already here, I really need a distraction from Josh; I can't afford to say anything that will blow my cover, and I know I can't handle those memories. Just seeing him brings those haunting memories back.

As I went to my seat, I saw in my peripheral vision that Josh went and sat in the back corner, probably trying not to draw any attention to himself. *Thank goodness.* The bell was about to ring and Connor was nowhere to be found. *Where the heck is he?*

I spent the rest of the day with Josh mumbling and showing him every class in the stinking school. I'm not bitter. He was a lot nicer than I remembered, I felt kind of bad, cause I was rude, but whatever. By the time I made it home, I was so exhausted with trying not to say something stupid and reveal myself while at the same time playing tour guide to the not so new kid. *I don't know how long I can keep this up without those memories coming back full blast. This is going to be a long night with probably no sleep.*

Chapter 6

Strong

"I'm home!" I yelled up the stairs to dad.

"Hey honey how was your first day back to school?" he said coming down the stairs.

"Interesting," I mumbled.

"Oh, how is that?" he gave me a hug and kiss on the forehead.

"I don't know dad, just new everything."

"Oh, so there's a new kid at school, let me guess . . . . A BOY!" he teased.

"How do you get that out of what I said?" I said agitated.

"Doll, look at your face, it's all red. I'm right and you know it!" he tousled my hair as he walked into the living room to watch the game; I rolled my eyes smiling, and walked upstairs.

★　★　★

Dad is my hero, even though we don't get along very well sometimes. After Ricky and I went our separate ways, I would have given up on trying to make friends or keeping my grades up, or anything if it weren't for him. He helped me keep my head up. He told me that I needed to be an example of grace,—forgiving someone when they don't deserve it. That was very hard for me during that time; I was a very angry little blonde. I wanted to hate Ricky and all those girls for stealing him from me. I wanted to hurt them, the cheerleaders who humiliated me and everyone else that egged it on. I did not think in terms of physically hurting them, but emotionally; like they all did to me. But I didn't hurt anyone through my anger and loneliness, which is not surprising really, considering my insecurities and shyness. I felt mostly hurt by Ricky, because he was the one who was supposed to be there for me when I needed him the most; he was supposed to be my best friend. I eventually learned to forgive Ricky, and over time to forget the past.

Dad is one of the strongest men I know, not in physical strength, but strength to deal with any situation. When my mom died, my brothers and I didn't take it very well. My oldest, Trey got very angry, he didn't want to deal with it, just like the rest of us, but he chose to sissy his way out of the pain by drinking. My second oldest brother, Ryan, just the opposite, didn't do anything. It was like he was in a coma but awake. He would go to school, come home barely eat anything, do his homework, and then go to sleep just to start all over again the next morning. Robby, my third brother was constantly asking why. "Why this? Why that? Why did this happen to us? I, on the other hand, was all of the above. I was angry. I was sad. I didn't understand why.

I was mostly like Ryan, not wanting to do anything, but sleep. I didn't eat except when Ricky or dad made me. Every once in a while the anger would ball up in my stomach and I would burst! Yelling and crying, asking God, why? In all of that and in the midst of his own pain, dad somehow kept us from totally falling apart. Most men would go crazy, but dad didn't, well at least not in front of us kids. He would tell us that it was hard, but we could make it with God's help, he said that we couldn't give up, because we needed to be examples, to show the world that God is our strength.

Dad did have a hard time though, just because he didn't do stupid things through his pain didn't mean that he still didn't cry, lose sleep or scream every once in a while. He would hide himself in his room for hours, but he never lost faith. At night I would hear him crying softly and praying a simple prayer—"God I know you are here, help the kids and me get through tomorrow. I love and trust you Lord. Amen."

Dear mommy,

I'm sorry I took it so badly, for not eating, and going through life like a zombie there for a while, I just missed you so much, and it was the most painful thing I've ever been through. I didn't know how to go through life without a mom, I wasn't ready to face the world alone, and I was only ten when you left. I still miss you every day. I breakdown at random times, please forgive me for acting this way, I know it would upset you if you knew how much we hurt sometimes. I just love you too much, and I know the boys and daddy do too.

P.S. You told me that I'm a lot like dad; the three S's you would say, short, shy and smiley. But he disagrees, he says I'm more like you, is that true?

—Your little bumble bee <3

Chapter 7

Crazy

She shook in horror as she sat in the middle of an angry mob. She was tangled in a web of lies. She waited for the first accuser to throw a heavy sharp rock. As she trembled on the ground, she could hear the angry mob yelling out hateful insults. She could only see blurred red faces and the movement of jaws clenching every time they went down from a syllable. She tried to think of a way to get out, but guilt from her little white lie kept taunting her to give up. In the back of her mind she knows that there's more to the story to the 'little white lies' but it's just not clear. She tried to stand to run, but the mob pushed her back to the ground. They started to throw her back and forth until finally she fell to the middle! She heard an angry deep voice yell, "Throw on three. "One . . . Two . . . Thr . . ."

I sat up, sweat streamed from my neck and face.

The house was quiet, except for the TV downstairs, *he must not have heard me, thank goodness. I really don't want him worrying about me.* I rolled over onto my side and hit my phone so that it lights up. Connor finally texted me back,

"Hey sorry I didn't text, my flight got delayed & my phone died . . . charger was in my bag . . . in the belly of the plane. :x"

I tripped down the stairs, and found Jen sitting on my couch eating cereal and watching *Tom and Jerry.*

Nice one . . .

This wasn't the first time.

"Morning sleepy head!" she,—like my dad—gets on my nerves in the morning. Not because it's them, but because they're *morning people.* I shuddered.

"Sup." I nodded.

"Girl, get dressed! What are you doing?"

"It's six thirty in the morning. School doesn't start 'till eight." I said in disgust. Mornings make me angry. "Why are you here?" I looked at her like she was crazy—well she is crazy, but I don't normally make it obvious that I think so. I would have laughed to myself, but it was too early.

"IDK just thought I'd stop by and help you get dressed." She said with a shrug.

"You labeled all my clothes. How can you help me more than that?"

She giggled; "Oh!" she rolled her eyes at me. The whole time we were talking my dad sat at the kitchen table, open mouthed staring at us.

"What?" Jen and I said sort of in unison, I was a little delayed from my lack of sleep. Her voice was a bit more chipper than my groan. When he realized we were asking him, he closed his mouth and shook his greying head.

"I will never understand teenage girls." He mumbled before spooning a huge mouthful of cereal into his mouth. He motioned to the empty seats across from him. "Come get yourself something to eat." He said with his mouth full. "Well; Blair, since Jenna already has food." He shook his head in humor and confusion. "Uh, Jenna, why are you here?" he continued.

"You always ask that!" she playfully tossed her hair.

"I just can't seem to get used to it I guess . . ." I laughed at them. Jen being totally oblivious to her random 'show ups' being odd and at my dad for his surprised reaction every time.

After breakfast I went upstairs to get in the shower and do all the things to get presentable. When ready, I walked down stairs in a simple pair of jeans from goodwill and a green tee that said 'peace out' I didn't feel like trying today and plus I know Jen's going to make me change. I decided last minute to add a vest to maybe keep her from making me change. I was wrong. Apparently there's more to fashion than just adding layers, who knew?

Jen was nodding her head as if to say 'walk back upstairs and change your clothes right now young lady!' She followed behind me as I sulked back up the stairs.

She took me to my own closet, and chewed me out, well In a Jenna sort of way.

"Those jeans are way to light to go with that dark shirt-" Yet again I mute her out.

When she was done with me I was wearing dark washed Bermuda shorts with black flats and the same tee. She slightly pulled back my long curled hair; enough to see the black dangly chain earrings. I tossed my head back and forth so the earrings would tickle my neck.

"Stop doing that you look like a doof." Jen teased.

On our way down the stairs I told her that Connor texted me back and should be home by now.

"Come on girls you're going to be late." Dad said totally interrupting our conversation.

Chapter 8

Stalker

As my dad drove up to the courtyard, I could see Josh in a bright green Zoo York shirt, sitting by the fountain.

"Bye dad, I love you." I said as Jen and I got out of the car.

"Bye honey."

"Bye Jay, thanks for the ride!" Jen smiled and waved.

"You bet!" he yelled through the rolled down window.

"Hey!" Josh said with his gorgeous smile as he saw us approaching. Yesterday was hard enough trying to keep up my lie of not knowing him, but today was going to be even harder . . . I was really hoping I could have avoided him today

"Hey." I said walking past him. Jenna turned and smiled at him.

"Hey wait," he walked up behind me and touched my shoulder. "Can you help me find homeroom? Yesterday I walked around forever trying to find it."

"Uh, sure, I guess."

Jen looked at me and then at Josh, "Uh, I'm going to go find Logan to stare at—I mean make fun of . . ." she blushed then skipped to the front door. I shook my head "gotta love her." I said half to myself.

"How are you this fine Tuesday morning?" he asked. *Really, do we have to talk? Just walk kid . . .*

"I'm okay."

"cool cool . . . you know usually people respond with the same question-" he interrupted himself by laughing.

"What's so funny?"

"Your dad just ran over that curb."

I rolled my eyes, "yeah he does that, I've kind of gotten over the embarrassment." I shrugged.

"Nah, it's not *too bad*, I've seen people more embarrassed than this." By the way he said that his eyes got darker, sad almost.

"Yeah . . . me too." I said under my breath.

"Yeah, I felt bad for her."

My head snapped up from where I was looking down at my hands playing with my book bag straps.

"What?"

I stared at him confused. He looked at me, almost just as confused. He must have been talking and I wasn't listening . . .

"You know that girl that you remind me of?"

I just looked away and started walking again.

"Well, she got really embarrassed one time in like eighth grade or something and even after whatever it was that happened, she got hassled for a long time . . ."

I stopped listening.

"Yeah . . ." My voice cracked, as I was brought back to the memories of my "stalker."

★   ★   ★

The same day of the so called "*fire drill*" I got an email making fun of me saying-

> "Nice display-double A!"
>   -Your biggest fans!

I kept getting emails saying the same kind of stuff, I didn't think much about all of them, just thought they were annoying and would go away after awhile. After two weeks of emails every day just being stupid and making fun of me, they started getting worse and coming more often. I started to email them back pleading for them to leave me alone, But that just made things worse. Dad wouldn't let me stay home from school, even though the teasing wasn't letting up, he said I was a big girl and could take it. Midway through February, a Facebook fan page was created for "AA." There were pictures and everything . . . My dad talked to the principal at school and somehow got the page down, but he still wouldn't let me stop going to school. By the end of February, I finally deleted my email address hoping at least the emails would stop. It was kind of silly for me not deleting it earlier, but my mom was the one who helped me set it up, and I didn't want to lose that part of her . . . After a while the teasing at school had faded out, but somehow the stalker got my number, so then the texts started coming. Mean, hateful texts. I changed my number, and that helped for a while until somehow they got my number again. By the beginning of March I had figured out that this person or persons were literally watching me, not just at school, but at home too. I could tell by some things they were saying. Like one day my dad and I were looking for batteries for his alarm clock and about an hour after we were looking and couldn't find any, I got a text from the unknown number saying, "U need double A batteries, they work the best." I didn't get it at first cause I thought they were just making fun of the whole "double A" thing. But once I got to thinking about it, no one else would have known that we were looking for batteries. After that, I stopped going to school. My physical health took a turn for the worse, my self-esteem was no longer existent, and I stopped eating again. Not because of my appearance, but because I was constantly sick from the stress and pain of the whole situation . . . After a couple of weeks, I started to calm down. I returned to school, and things started looking up, no more teasing constantly from everyone at school and no more annoying emails and texts, but I still felt watched. I could feel eyes on me at all times, and I'm not talking about from all the students, but from someone *watching* me . . . Then the letters started coming. They went from hateful to sickly sweet. And they always ended with: "-a changed fan."

I started getting really mad and scared all over again. I told my dad, but he didn't do anything because he thought that they sounded like genuine apologies. But those eyes were still watching me . . . by the beginning of April I refused to go to school, nobody could make me go! After three months of the roller coaster of emotions and terrible health, I couldn't take it anymore. I was tired and physically worn out. I went to the hospital a couple of times during that period of my life because I would subconsciously hurt myself in the middle of the night while I was dreaming. My dad and I couldn't take anymore, so we moved across the country to California.

"Blair, Blair, BLAIR!"

"WHAT!" I screamed as I spun in a complete circle, thinking something was behind me. Josh burst out laughing.

"There's nothing there."

"Oh . . ."

"You were staring off into space." His laughter slowed.

"Oh. Yeah I do that a lot . . ." I felt my face get hot. The bell rang as we walked inside.

★   ★   ★

I tried to pay attention to the teacher, but I was still thinking about my stalker. I tried to push the memories out of my mind for so long that I even made myself believe that I forgot them. I haven't, they're still there. And with someone from that era of my past coming back into my life, brings those momeories flying back into my mind. Oh how I thought I moved on from them, but I guess I haven't . . . That unwanted crave of wonder was slowly creeping up on me again. *I have to figure out who it was; it's going to drive me crazy*. Before I moved, I tried to find out more about the "stalker." The email address was an unregistered account that was made on the same day my first email came. There was no trace of emails to anyone, but me. One day I even walked to the house that the return address on the letters were from, but it was vacant. An old lady by the name of Helen Clarkson once lived there. She had moved to a nursing home about three years before the *fire drill*. She had no children and her neighbors on the right were a couple with a newborn, and on her left an old man whose grandchildren were all older.

I got a package around the end of March, about three months after the *fire drill*. It had a card shaped like a heart with a band-aid taped to it that said:

Forgive them for they know not what they have done . . .—a changed fan

That's when my dad started to see that something was really bothering me. It was getting really bad, so by the time April came, my dad decided that it was too much on me and that we needed to move. He said it would be good to leave, "This house reminds me too much of your mother." So that's when we decided to move.

The reason we picked the sunny hills of Cali was because we couldn't bear not living by the beach, but we also wanted to try something new by living near the hills.

The beach was our paradise. On the days I didn't go to school my dad would sometimes take me to the beach and we'd spend the whole day together, either lying in the soft sand, soaking in the sun, people watching, drifting in and out of sleep or splashing each other in the salty water.

★　　★　　★

After school dad picked up Jen and me, and took us back to our house.

As we walked in the door I heard a deep voice yelling at the TV, "Run baby run—go—go, TOUCH DOWN! WOOHOO!" Then big hands clapping loudly.

"Dad; who's in our house?" I whispered eyes wide. Jen was standing still next to me eyes even wider.

"A burglar watching the game." He winked.

"OHMYGOSH!" I screamed as I saw my brother Ryan sitting in the living room. I haven't seen any of my brothers in like . . . forever! Trey left for college about five years ago (he's twenty-six now, ten years older than me) and got married about two years ago. He comes and visits on holidays and some in the summer but, other than that, I don't get to see him much. The other two are the same way; Ryan left for college about three years ago, Robby went when we moved. So, you see that I'm younger by quite a few years.

What are you doing here?" I asked while being smothered in a huge bear hug from Ryan.

"I was on my way to Mexico for my senior project." He laughed. "So I stopped by."

"Sweet. So, how's your senior year going?" I asked smiling a huge smile.

"Good. I'm just glad I'm almost done." I noticed Jen standing beside me.

"Oh, this is my best friend Jen."

"Nice to meet you Jen." Ryan polity grabbed her hand with both of his and shook it.

We laughed and talked until it was way past midnight, Jenna had gone home after dinner. It was good to get my mind off the "stalker" and Josh. I finally had to excuse myself, it was getting late and I had homework.

"Well, I better follow; this old thing needs his sleep." Dad joked.

"There are sheets and blankets in the closet you can use on the couch." I said to Ryan.

"Thanks."

"Nighty night," I said as I walked upstairs to my bedroom.

"Good night doll."

"Good night," Ryan echoed.

When I got upstairs I sat on my bed and grabbed my bag and pulled out my books and started on my homework. I was twirling my pencil in between my fingers while I read and me being Miss graceful, dropped the pencil and it rolled under my bed. I hopped off and pulled up the bed skirt, I froze. I had completely forgotten that I put the box under the bed. I don't even know why I kept those awful memories all this time. There sat an old tattered converse shoe box that had layers of torn duck-tape from sleepless nights of trying to figure out the puzzle of what's inside. That ugly old box was full of the stuff from the "stalker." I sat staring at it for a long time until finally I decided to open it, adding another layer to the torn tape. I slowly opened the lid, dreading what was inside, but quickly shut it for there was no reason for me to relive the past.

"Gah, Blair why are you doing this to yourself?"

Is this really something I want to do?

"I can't stand unsolved puzzles. This is driving me nuts!"

I guess the only way to solve a puzzle is to lay out the pieces and put it together.

As I reopened and looked through the box with shaky hands, there were tons of letters, printed emails, papers with text messages that I had copied, and a lot of other random stuff *the stalker* had sent me. I started to read through some of the emails, *how could someone be so mean?* The things that they said were so off the wall, but creepy and annoying at the same time. How would they know so much about me?—I never talked to anyone.

There's something missing.

"What do I need to find to solve this puzzle?"

What am I missing?

"Ricky?"

NO, He may have left me but he would never do something like that. He's not that kind of person. Okay Blair, focus!

I had forgotten that the emails were from "skaterfreak21". I know it's a big piece in the puzzle, but I can't find were it fits. I kept reading the clues until I finally had to stop, because I started freaking myself out. I was mentally exhausted and having stayed up so late with Ryan, I really needed to go to sleep.

★   ★   ★

Dear mommy,

The memories I want to disappear seem to never leave my mind, but the memories of you, the memories I fight so hard to hold on to, I feel are slipping away from my grasp. Not just the little ones like you tucking me in at night or the times I would

41

sit on your bathroom counter and watch you curl your long blonde hair. But also the huge ones like my 10th birthday or our last Christmas together. Is it that I'm trying so hard to forget the bad memories that my mind is holding onto them even tighter? Or is there something I need to do in order for my brain to let them go? I need your help mama; you were so good at helping me straighten out the difficult and confusing things. I know you're watching me and I hope I'm making you smile, that's all I want to do, is make you smile.

I love you mommy, and miss you more than any words could say, not even the greatest poet could describe how much I miss you.

-your little bumble bee < 3

Chapter 9

Eerie

The hall way is dark, unusually dark, Except for a dim blinking green light from the fire alarm at the very end, above the window. The white brick walls are lined with gray beat up lockers some have the usual relationship statuses with graffiti mixed in and others are touched with rust. It feels like they are closing in on me.

Have I been here before?

As I tiptoe down the eerie, inky black hall way I see the shadow lurking before me. As the car passes, its head lights dance across the walls bringing the shadow's form to life.

I can feel it.

It isn't the innocent shadow of a child, or the huge shadow that would come from a monster, it really isn't all that scary . . . if it wasn't following you.

I stoop behind a classroom door; there are posters on all the walls, shelves of books and more books.

My eighth grade science class . . .

I feel a presence behind me, boring into the back of my head. I slowly turn around not wanting to see the eyes that stare.

I jump! There is a body so still that it looks as though it isn't real . . .

We stand here in the silence for what feels like an eternity, glaring at each other with fierce eyes, tearing each other apart. I hear the shadow's heavy footsteps, announcing its presence, shaking my focus from the eyes in front of me. I squeeze my eyes shut; as tightly as I can as if to take me to another world. Away from it. When I open my eyes, I can see a little bit better from my eyes adjusting. The body before me is a model skeleton. I exhale realizing I have been holding my breath.

The footsteps are getting farther down the long school hall way. I creep out of my eighth grade science classroom, and get on all fours to crawl past the window, just in case it turns around.

The footsteps stop.

A squeak from tennis shoes turning to quickly skid against the linoleum floors. I gasp. The shadow saw me mid crawl, and makes a dash in my direction. I jump up as fast as I possibly can and run down the hall way that T's at the window. I choose right, knowing that it will lead to the cafeteria then to the front door. My legs are wobbling, I'm off balance, but I won't stop.

Confusion. Anxiety. Terror. Pours on me like pounding rain. It presses against my chest; it feels like it's caving in. I puff out my chest to make the feeling go away. It feels like I'm running in a dark tunnel, though it's only a hall way that hundreds of students walk every day, including me. How long have I been running? Did I pass the cafeteria? No. that's impossible, you **can't** pass it, I would run into a literal brick wall. *I keep going and going, the heavy footsteps still in a fast pace behind me.* Maybe if I keep running I'll get too tired and collapse.

But that's giving up.

A second voice in my head says. You're right. I can't give up!

For some reason it feels good to run. The deep aching breaths of cold air, the pounding rhythm of my feet hitting the hard floor, the power I feel in my thighs and calves, it all gives me a since of realness.

I feel the shadow creeping up behind me. I push through my toes even harder against the floor, yearning to get to the front door.

Finally the cafeteria! I Begin to get excited, my run turns to a skip. Only a few more steps!

I trip in my excitement, the shadow takes the advantage and dives forward grabbing my heel! I'm reaching for anything to help me, a chair, table leg, ANYTHING! My fingers dig into the floor finding a crack, my nails break too short and I scream out in pain! The shadow watches me fight against it, until it grabs the back of my knee . . . .

Yet again I woke up sweating from a horrible dream, this time screaming. It was worse. **I** was in the dream. Not only that, but I've had that dream before. I would dream it every night after I found out that someone was actually watching and following me.

"BLAIR! Are you okay? What's wrong? Are you hurt? Is someone in here?" Ryan blurted out all at once, with a horrified look on his face.

"Yes—sorry . . ."

"Blair, talk to me what's wrong?"

"I'm fine—Really. Just a bad dream . . ." I forced a smile.

"Should I tell dad?"

"**No**! I mean no." he looked puzzled. "Look, ever since I had *those dreams* a couple of years ago, dad gets all worried every time I have a common nightmare. Really everything is fine."

"Well if you say so . . ." I smiled at him, this time not faking it. I was genuinely happy to see him.

"Hey can I take you to school today? I'll be gone by the time you get home."

"Okay yeah that's cool, but I can't be late."

"Okay we won't be." he said trying to be convincing. *Yeah right, this family is never on time.*

"Okay," I giggled knowing I was going to be late. "I'm going to hop in the shower and get ready."

"Mmkay. Hey by the way that chick is down stairs eating our food and watching TV should I be worried?" He asked bewildered.

"Oh ha-ha that's just Jen, she randomly does that."

"Uh? Okay . . ." he walked out of my room mumbling something about kids being all weird in Cali.

Chapter 10

Shy

Ryan took me to breakfast and then to school. I was *late.* I had to walk to the office to tell the old, withered creepy lady that I was here and late. On the way, I passed the gym where I saw sweaty boys playing basketball. I noticed that one of them was Josh, so I stopped and watched him dribble the ball ever so gracefully up and down and then pass it quickly to his teammate. I broke away from my stare and continued to walk toward the office. The old lady gave me a tardy slip to fill out; I handed it back to her with a forced smile and walked to class. Class was almost finished, so I decided to sit in the hall and finish the homework from last night. The bell rang as I was putting my books in my locker; I started to walk to my next class, but stopped when I heard my name being called from the opposite end of the hall.

"Blair! Blair!" I spun around so fast I almost fell down It was Connor!

"Oh my goodness HEY!" I squealed as I gave him a huge hug.

"Wow you look great! He said with a shy smile, I haven't seen you since this summer, how ya been?"

"Aw thanks" I said embarrassed. "You don't look so bad yourself." I giggled while examining him from head to toe. "I've been okay. I've been really distracted these past couple of days with school starting back and everything, and mad at you for not being here!" He grinned. "Where have you been, you should have at least been here yesterday! I've texted you like thirty times." *I could have used him as a distraction from Josh on the first day.*

"Because our flight was so delayed, my mom let me sleep and get settled back in, I mean we don't really do anything anyway."

"Aw I bet that was nice, well I'm glad you got all rested up." I smiled at him. "There are three new kids this year." I informed.

"Yeah that's what Will told me when I walked in today." he said with a humorous look.

"What is that supposed to mean?" I urged.

"Well, supposedly the girl is hot, he told me he had dibs and walked away." He chuckled "and then I heard a group of girls talking about some new kid Josh, and from what I could tell they obviously thought he was hot too."

I laughed. "Our school is so small that when a couple of attractive new people come the hormones start raging."

He laughed and put his arm around my shoulders. Once Connor got used to me, he never left my side. I mean that metaphorically—well I guess that's also true physically. We have a different relationship. Jenna is always saying; "you guys would be like the cutest couple ever!" It's not like that though. People think that just because he sometimes might put his arm around me or playfully hold my hand that it's more than what it is. He's like another brother.

"So, how about you and I go get some coffee after school?"

"Yeah that sounds great; I want to hear all about your trip." I said with a smile. We had arrived at my class without noticing. "Oh and don't forget our movie night tomorrow, first Friday of the season; you can't miss it!"

"Definitely. I'll be there! Bye B." He said grinning. He has called me "B" since I first met him. He would say things like "hey you" and "chick" I finally figured out that he couldn't remember my name so I gave him a little hint, "it starts with a "B"

"Bye" I said as I twinkled my fingers. I giggled at myself as I began to look back to my first day here:

★   ★   ★

When I walked in to my new private school in ninth grade, I was surprised to see that it was a small school, way smaller than the public school I went to in Florida. I didn't know where to go, so I asked some girl, who looked like she was a living manikin—I later learned that was Mandy—where the office was and she looked at me like I was trash and walked off! What a great way to start a day, being ticked off. Ever since then, she's not been my favorite person. So, I tried again with a tall dark headed freckle faced boy who wore glasses and talked like a hick, which means he must have moved here, because people don't talk like that here. I asked him where the office was, "Daawwn the haaall" he said very slowly dragging out his vowels. *Wow that did a lot of good there are like fifty hallways.* So I started to walk down the hall with the fewest people. I accidentally bumped into a semi tall, blonde headed boy, who still had his baby face.

"Oh my goodness I am so sorry!" I exclaimed as I bent down to pick up the books that I had knocked out of his hands.

"It's okay it happens all the time." He said with a cute shy smile.

"I'm Blair."

"Oh, you must be the new girl, I'm Connor."

"Yeah." I blushed, I didn't like standing out. It was like I had a huge flashing sign over my head that said "new kid!"

"Didn't you move from Florida?"

"Yeah? How do you know that?" I gave him a suspicious look.

He looked down trying to hide his face, red from blushing.

"My dad is friends with the principal here and told me that there was going to be a new girl from Florida, in my grade."

"Oh that makes sense," I giggled.

"We don't really get very many new kids in the high school department so; the guys might be overly excited about you." I giggled.

"Oh my . . . I doubt that. Um, could you help me find my next class, I'm really lost." I asked biting the right side of my lower lip, feeling bad for asking. His face lit up.

"Sure." For the rest of the day he showed me where everything was and told me funny stories about things that happened at different places in the school. He also introduced me to Jen.

★   ★   ★

I snapped out of my "blast to the past" when I saw a post it note taped to my desk, it read:

Meet me in the gym after school. ☺
Jen

I giggled at the smiley and stuffed the "post it" in my pocket.

★   ★   ★

After school I walked to the gym to meet Jen, she was standing by the door, talking to a couple of girls. Her posture was straight and she bobbed when she talked, making her ponytail swing back in forth.

What a dork. I teased in my mind. I tapped her on her shoulder and she turned around.

"Hey, I got your note, what's up?"

"Oh I was just seeing if you needed a ride home, since your brother dropped you off this morning." Before I could answer someone interrupted.

"Actually I was hoping I could take her home today." I turned around to find Josh standing there grinning from ear to ear. I literally stood there shocked, and before I could refuse, Jenna answered for me.

"You know what, I just thought about something, I'm not going to be able to take you home today B, so that would be great Josh if you could do that." She flashed him a smile.

"But—" I tried to interject, but Jen stepped on my foot to stop me.

"Well great, glad I could help." He threw Jenna a quick wink. Jenna kissed me on the check and scurried off, ponytail bobbing back and forth.

"So I was thinking we could go by that little café place not too far from here, on the way, that is if you want to."

"Uh, look that's really nice of you but I can just call my dad or brother and they can come get me." I forced a quick smile and started to walk away but he grabbed my shoulder.

"Please Blair, to be honest I don't know how to get there and I heard they have the best fraps, and I've been craving one since I got here." He tried to look pitiful. I rolled my eyes and chuckled. I thought a moment and bit my lower lip trying to decide what to do. *I mean he doesn't seem to remember me and . . . he is cute . . .*

"I guess-" He smiled. "-But only because I'm a nice person, and really do need a ride."

"Great!"

We walked to his car and he opened the door for me, as I bent down to get in the car, he stopped me.

"Wait." he said touching my shoulder. I stepped back and stated to wobble, losing my balance slightly.

"You ok?" he asked with humor in his eyes.

"Yeah, I'm fine." *Wow B . . . way to be a klutz . . .*

"Did you seriously almost fall just from stepping backwards?" he asked on the brink of laughing. I looked at him through my hair.

Shrugging, "guilty."

"You are the only person I know that could almost fall just by standing still." He chuckled.

I rolled my eyes and stood up straight trying to look confident. He cleared off the seat and helped me in, and winked.

"Put your seatbelt on." I rolled my eyes and did what he said.

"So, there's actually a reason I wanted to take you home today."

My body stiffened knowing what was coming . . . *Dangit Blair! Of course he knows! You are so stupid for going out with him like this . . .*

"I wanted to celebrate." My eyes shot up, I looked at him confused. "I made the basketball team." He grinned a huge cheesy smile. *Well that was not what I was thinking he was going to say . . .*

"Ohh." Was all I managed to say.

He looked over at me amused, "I was nervous because they already had tryouts over the summer, so there was a huge possibility that I wouldn't make it."

"Well that's cool, congrats. But um, what does taking me home have to do with that?" he gripped the steering wheel and chuckled.

"You are the only person I know here." *So he does know . . .* "And I wanted to celebrate with someone that's not in my family. I've been around them **way** to much lately with the move and all." He shrugged.

"Uh huh . . ." I looked out the window, "Look Josh," I started to try and explain why I lied to him about not knowing him, but he interrupted.

"Uh, don't forget I have no idea where I'm going, you're going to have to tell me."

"Oh yeah, sorry turn right at the light and it'll be on your left across the street from the park. You'll see the tables outside."

"Sweet. Thanks for coming out with me today, basketball is sort of important to me, so it means a lot that you were nice enough to hang out with a stranger like me today." He flashed me his perfect smile . . . . *so he doesn't know . . . dang I'm confused . . .*

"Uh, yeah, no problem. Why is this so important to you?"

"Uh I guess because sports is all I know. Without them I wouldn't know what to do with myself." he laughed at himself and continued, "Especially now that I moved. My dad used to say that I inherited the sports freak-ness from him."

I froze. *Sports freak?*

My mind jumped from coincidence to conclusion. *That sounds an awful lot like "skaterfreak"* Before I got myself worked up, I decided in that split second to ask him a question to test him to see if he **was** my stalker.

"Did you ever skate?" He looked at me confused.

"Like skateboard?" I nodded. "Uh yeah actually, I got really into it a couple of years ago, why?" I ignored his why question and asked one of my own.

"What's your favorite number?" *Ok, if it's twenty-one then I know it is him.* His confused expression turned to amused.

"Uh, Five I guess. Why?" I exhaled.

Ok this is a good sign. "I don't know; I just want to get to know you a little better." I lied. "Now, you ask me a question." *Nice save B . . .*

"Okay? Umm, what's your favorite color?" he asked.

"Blue." We had arrived at *Coco's* and got out of the car; we walked in and ordered our drinks.

"It's your turn to ask a question," he teased as we waited at the counter.

"Did you play basketball in Florida?"

"Yes. Let's see, what can I ask you? Hum? Do you . . . have a, boyfriend?" I froze. *Did not expect that at all . . .*

"Uh, no."

"Oh?" he looked pleased. He grabbed both drinks from the counter and walked over and sat down at the table in the corner by the door.

"Don't get any ideas." I rolled my eyes and tried to stay calm, "Isn't it my turn to ask a question?"

"Yeah I think . . ." he sounded wounded. *This week has been so strange . . .*

"Ok then, what was your jersey number?" *please don't be twenty-one! Please don't be Twenty-one!*

"Twenty-one"

"What!" *This has to be a crazy coincidence! I know Josh was popular, but he seemed like an all around good guy, why would he want to harass me like that? NO, B this is crazy it wasn't him! It couldn't have been!* I argued with myself long enough for Josh to notice.

"What is your email address?"

"Whoa, Whoa," he threw his hands up next to his head. "Isn't it my turn to ask a question," he teased.

"Oh yeah, sorry," my voice sounded weak.

"Umm, what do you like to do in your free time?"

"Go to the beach, mall, really anything as long as my friends are with me." I said short. "Ok so what is your email address?"

"Why so urgent?" he laughed. "Well I have two. The first one is Josh@Josh.net—"

"Wow! How original." I teased. He rolled his eyes at me and continued.

"And the second one is-"

"Blair?" asked an angry voice behind me.

I turned around and saw Connor standing there.

Oh my gosh, Blair, how could you be such a jerk and forget about Connor!

"Oh crap! I totally forgot! I am so sorry, how can I make it up to you?" I pleaded to Connor.

"Whatever B-" he stopped, "Blair." He corrected. "Just have fun with **him**, whoever he is." He glared at Josh and stormed out of the building.

I started to feel my eyes water, but sucked it back in and tried to chase after him, but it was too late he had already zoomed off.

"Can you please take me home?" I whispered to Josh.

When I got home I tried to call Connor, his mom picked up and said he was still out. I said "thank you" and hung up. I started to cry. I know maybe crying is a little over dramatic, but I couldn't lose Connor, he was my best friend! He had done so much for me.

I started to remember my favorite moment with him. We were at the mall around Christmas time, the mall was packed and we had to get last minute shopping done for our families. It was almost impossible to walk without trampling some random little kid that was trying to find his mom, so he could take a picture with Santa. I had to pee like no tomorrow, but the restroom was on the opposite end of the mall at the food court. It would take me a lifetime to get over there.

"Hey I need to go to the restroom; I'll meet you in the food court!" I yelled over the crowd.

"Okay, don't hurt yourself!" He yelled back.

"I'll try not to!" I teased. I shuffled my way to the bathroom, trying not to hurt anyone, I didn't succeed. I tripped over a wheelchair and hit some old guy in the gut—oops. I finally got to the bathroom, but had to wait for like an hour! I was dancing like a little kid. I made it thankfully! When I got out, I saw Connor standing there with two cups in his hands.

"I thought we were meeting in the food court."

"Yeah, but I could tell this was going to take a while, so I went ahead and got some hot chocolate, and came back here so we'd be sure to find each other."

It's the little things about Connor that I love. Things like that. He didn't have to get hot chocolate; he could have just waited for me.

After we sat and drank our cocoa, he decided to take me on the merry-go-round to get away from the crowds. Connor is always doing random stuff like that. He is always there for me, thinking of the things that I would never think to do or say. He is my shoulder to cry on and the friend to hang out with when literally there's nothing to do.

It's stupid for me to cry, I know it will pass, but it just hurt to see Connor so mad at me.

★   ★   ★

I did my homework and then went straight to bed. When I was almost asleep, I remembered that I didn't get Josh's second email address. I hopped out of bed and started to call him.

"Hello?"

"Hey it's Blair."

"Oh! Hey, how did it go with Connor?"

"It didn't *go;* he had his mom lie to me saying he wasn't there. Sorry about leaving so fast."

"It's okay, I understand." He said sincerely.

"Thanks. But, um, I never got your other email address; I wanted to forward something to you."

"Oh yeah, its skaterfreak21."

I froze . . . . The phone slipped out of my hand, I scrambled to pick it up and mumbled something that was supposed to be "bye" and hit the 'end' button.

Chapter 11

Sorry

I woke up soaked in sweat. I had the same dream as the night before, the one in the hallway, except this time I knew subconsciously that the shadow belonged to Josh . . .

After I hung up with Josh last night, I barely slept a wink. I don't understand why someone would want to do that to me, much less him. I never did anything or talked to anyone, especially not to him and his friends. I kept to myself, I didn't even try to look at Josh when Taylor (head cheerleader and Josh's on again off again girlfriend) was around. Ok, I bumped in to Josh one time by accident in sixth grade. All I said to him was *sorry* and then I ran, (yes, I know, I ran like a little pansy.) but why would Taylor and her friends want to prank me like that? I still don't know and probably will never know. And why would Josh freak me out by writing those stupid letters and emails making fun of me and then actually watching me? None of it makes any sense?

When I walked in to school the next morning, I saw Josh coming straight for me from down the middle hallway. I didn't want to see him; I was too upset about the

Connor thing and mad at Josh for sending me all those stupid letters, and not to mention scared to death that my once stalker, somehow ended up all the way across the country in the very same school as me! So, I turned left down the deserted hall lined with lockers to try to get away from him

"Blair! Blair!"

Leave me alone!

"I know you can hear me! Why did you hang up on me last night?"

"I'm in a hurry I'll explain later!" I said angrier and shakier than I meant for it to come out.

"Whoa? Looks like someone woke up on the wrong side of the bed this morning." he laughed, mockingly behind me, closer than I wanted.

"Just shut up and leave me alone! I told you I would explain later." I started to cry and walked off with loud heavy footsteps, leaving Josh open mouth and stunned in his tracks.

"Whoa, whoa, whoa hold up! What the heck is wrong with you?" he said as he chased after me. "I would appreciate it if you didn't yell at me, until I know what I did to deserve it." I spun around and glared at him through wet eyes. "Wait, are you okay?" his expression softened looking genuinely concerned.

My hands went into a tight fist, I felt my nails digging into my palms. "I would appreciate it if you would leave me alone." I whispered through clenched teeth, trying to hide my husky voice.

"Okay, okay. Fine if that's what you want." He sounded hurt.

"Yes." I whispered as I ran off to class. Okay maybe I should have played it cool, but how could I when he freaking stalked me? And I don't even know if he recognizes me for sure . . . what if he does? What if he's known all along and that's why he keeps trying to talk to me . . . I started to hyperventilate. Cold sweats broke out and I was shaking uncontrollably. Tears streamed down my face. *Why did he have to come here? Follow me? I thought I was done with all of that . . . I need Jenna and Connor . . .*

★   ★   ★

Later that day at lunch I saw Connor, I tried to talk to him, but he just shrugged me off and walked away. It stung. So I walked outside alone to the stone picnic tables and sat with Jen.

"Hey cutie." Jen giggled.

"Hey . . ." my voice trailed off.

"So I was thinking that this weekend we should go shopping. There's a huge sale on Butler St-"

"Uh huh that sounds fun." Jen kept planning the "spree" while I was freaking out about Josh and my stalker being the same person. *This is really frightening me. I've got to talk this out . . . I know I can't talk to Connor because he's pissed at me.* She stopped talking. "Sweetie, are you okay?"

"Oh umm, yeah" she pondered for a second and then continued talking about whatever it was she was talking about. I started to drift back into my own issues.

I wonder if I could maybe tell Jen . . . would she listen, or even care . . . can I trust her? We've never talked about anything like this before . . . I mean I told her about the fire drill, but I didn't say anything about my stalker . . . I didn't want to go there again. Ever. Should I tell her that it's my problem or try the whole bogus 'I have a friend with a problem' story? Well if I go with the 'bogus friend' thing I know Jen won't catch on, but is that really being honest?-

"Hey, Jen?" I asked as I looked up from where I was poking my salad with my fork, totally interrupting whatever she was talking about.

"-Uh yeah?" She looked up with her bright confused eyes. "What's up?"

"Uh can I tell you something—well more like ask you." My eyes fell back to my salad.

"Of course!" she said sincerely.

"Uh . . ." *how can I start this?*

"Um well, I'm not okay . . . I'm actually kind of freaking out . . ."

"Oh sweetie." She frowned. "What's wrong?" her huge brown eyes told me she was listening.

"I-I don't really know where to start . . ." I paused trying to think of how in the heck I was going to tell her this.

"You know how I moved here?"

"Yes . . ." her voice trailed off. *Obviously she knows that, B.*

"And you know what happened to me in eighth grade, the reason why I moved?"

"Yeah, those horrible girls pulled a prank on you and the teasing never stopped, right?"

"Yeah . . . well there's more . . ." I stopped again. "Well, the teasing and harassment at school was hard enough and impossible to get away from, but it followed me home too, I started getting these crazy annoying e-mails picking at me and making fun of my *smaller physique-"* I couldn't help but laugh at myself for that one. "I thought it was just something that I could ignore and move on from, like the teasing at school, but it just kept getting worse." I stabbed my salad with my black plastic fork, and watched it bend till it snapped. As I told Jen all the details of my stalker I felt a million miles away from the cold hard stone seat that I was sitting on. It was like I was back in Florida in my old room sitting at my computer. The overwhelming emotion crashed into me like a tidal wave. "If that's not enough, I felt watched and things started to get even more personal and I started having these horrible graphic dreams. I mean there was this sick, insane person out there watching me!" I looked at Jenna to see if she was completely freaked out yet. She was. She reached her hand out and placed it over top of mine; she gave me a reassuring look and squeezed my hand tenderly.

I could feel the blood rushing to my cheeks as my face was starting to heat up. My hands were shaking, breaking out in cold sweats. My chest was aching from trying to hold back angry sobs.

"Then one day I got a text that was more than I could handle, I didn't just **feel** watched, I **was** being watched." I fell silent, horrified. Jen just stared at me with huge eyes. "But if that wasn't enough, later that day when I went outside, there were AA batteries in the mailbox."

Jen and I shuddered at the same time. My knees started wobbling; I couldn't hold my own weight. This is why I refused to remember; the eerie feeling I got when I first saw the batteries always comes crashing back onto me every time I relive that part of the past . . . I couldn't do or say anything. I caught my breath and finished, "So that's when I stopped going to school, after awhile things faded, and I tried going back to school again, but I never stopped feeling eyes on me, and the dreams never stopped either. I even started hallucinating, seeing shadows following me constantly.

After a while things calmed down again, totally this time, I was still terrified, but I tried to move on till the written letters came . . . this time, instead of mean insults they were nice, *too* nice. Finally I couldn't take it anymore, so we moved. I forgot about it all after I met you and Con, until Josh showed up . . ."

"Why do I have a feeling that this new Josh kid is a creep?" My body trembled even more in my seat. "Because he is." I didn't plan on crying, but it just happened. Jen got up from her seat across from me and ran around and sat beside me and hugged me tightly, stroking my hair.

"Now, now it's going to be okay, we'll take care of it." She patted my arm. "Are you going to be okay?" I didn't say anything . . . the truth is I don't know if I'm going to be okay, I mean the kid freaking was at my house, watching me through my window! I looked up at her face, it was sincere. She reached across the table and grabbed her silver clutch, and grabbed a tissue. She plotted my eyes and wiped the streaming makeup from my cheeks and chin.

"There." She smiled tenderly. "That's better."

"Thank you . . ." *at least I got it out . . . I know she won't tell anyone . . . oh how I need Connor . . .*

"I'll call your dad—"

"NO!" I yelled, "You can't."

"Okay, I won't say a word. But B?"

"Yeah?"

"You need to tell him, especially since Josh is here. For your safety."

I looked at her and nodded, not knowing if I should listen to her or not. We got up from our table and gathered our stuff and walked back inside.

"Hey girl, are you okay? I gotta split here and go to gym."

"Yeah I'm fine, try not to kill anyone with that mad swing of yours with a tennis racket."

"Hey now, I may not be athletic or very graceful, but at least I look good. Okay." she snapped her fingers and did her famous wink. We laughed and went our separate ways.

The thing with Josh was still bothering me as I walked in to class. Connor was sitting in his usual seat and I normally sit next to him, but today I'm not so sure.

"Hey Con," I said timidly, trying to read how he would react.

Nothing

I sat down next to him anyways and got out my books, grabbed my journal and a pen and did what I needed to do most . . .

Dear mommy,

Connor's not talking to me so I'm coming to you, I really need someone to talk to right now. All this mess with Josh is just really weighing on me; this is a time when I could really use my mommy. Dad is always teasing me about having boy issues, but this goes beyond that and I know that you would have just the right things to say to me. Remember when Trey first went to college and he started acting all different. I didn't really understand what was happening then, all I saw was my brother changing. He was hurting himself and that hurt me. You told me "Never lose who you are because of something that someone else has done." I need that voice right now encouraging me to stand up and face what I am so used to running from.

Mommy I need you!

-B

When the last bell rang, I hurriedly shuffled out of class to the parking lot in a blur, only to find Josh standing by my car waiting for me. Oh! *I can't do this!*

"Can I ask you a question without you getting all mad?" Josh asked as he walked closer to me, looking like a little kid waiting to be told his punishment. I looked him over once and then said with a shaky voice.

"You just did." I rolled my eyes in a nervous glare, trying to not be obvious that he really was scaring me.

"What?" he looked confused.

"You asked if you could ask a question." I shifted my weight and crossed my arms over my chest in annoyance.

A light bulb went off—"Oh." I glared at him.

"What do you want?" I asked impatiently.

"I just want to know what I did wrong earlier today." He pouted. I couldn't stop from feeling sorry for him, I mean he just moved and only had one friend; me. Then all the sudden I go ballistic on him! *But he disserved it!*

"Look, I'm sorry I took it out on you," I uncrossed my arms and shoved them into my jeans pockets. I was just trying to get him to go away! "I just figured out . . . some very unpleasant news last night and it kind of . . . hit me hard, and err, I need to sort it all out." I had to choose my words carefully so that I didn't give off too much information.

"Oh . . . so I'm guessing Connor called you back?"

"Uh . . . Yeah" I lied, "Look Connor didn't deserve for me to do that to him, he would never forget about me like I forgot about him. I know I hurt him really bad and that makes me feel like a piece of dirt! But I have to go!" I started to walk around the car but he stopped me. I stared at him with furious eyes.

"I understand," he reached out and touched my arm, and dropped when he saw me flinch away. "So why did you hang up on me last night?"

"Umm, I'm not supposed to be on the phone after 11:00 and my dad almost walked in on me talking to you." *I have never lied this much in my life . . .*

"Wow your parents are really strict."

"My parent." I corrected. I felt a lump forming in my throat, but I pushed it down before he could see.

"Oh, I'm sorry." He looked deep into my eyes like he was searching for something. It scared me.

"I have to go." My voice was husky as I broke eye contact. I froze when he started talking again.

"Every time I talk to you, you remind me of the girl I knew in middle school." I shuddered. *Either he knows it's me or is about to put the last puzzle piece together.*

I threw my hands up, giving up, but to him it looked like I was saying it was the stupidest thing I'd ever heard. "Ha-ha that's impossible! I've never even stepped foot on Florida ground."

Something was bothering him, and it had something to do with me, not the California me here, but the old Florida me.

"I know, but I can't help but think of her when I look at you." I started to open the door to leave but a thought acquired to me . . .

"If you don't mind me asking, why do you always look like something is bothering you when 'that girl' is brought up?"

He didn't answer right away. "I always saw something in her," he paused. "She was so quiet I only heard her speak once, she said 'sorry' and then ran away." A sad chuckle left his lips, he looking away. The mood got serious again when he looked down at me; it made me squirm I didn't like him this close looking deep inside of me. "But I could see she was . . . different. I tried to do some research on her-"

"You did research on m-her?" this conversation was getting too far out of my comfort zone.

"Yeah, but I never got very far, something would always get in the way, like my girlfriend would always happen to walk in or the computer would freeze up, but the strangest one was the page in the phonebook where her dad's name was supposed to be, was torn out."

I almost started to cry, fright crept up from the bottom of my gut, and I felt nauseous. *Why would he go to so much trouble, to find out stuff about me just so he could just turn around and make me feel horrible? Or scare me? What kind of sick person would do that!* I blinked back the tears so he wouldn't see me.

He looked as though he were far away, "After the *fire drill* I didn't see much of her, when I did happen to see her she seemed really . . . scared. And then all of a sudden she never came back to school."

"What kind of person would stalk someone so they could make m-her feel like crap? Why would you scar her? Till the point she moved! Why would **you** do that?!" I jabbed at him.

"Wait a minute! Who said I was trying to make her feel like crap? I wasn't trying-"

"Oh don't make it sound like you are so innocent. When it's obvious you aren't."

"Whoa chickadee, why so defensive? What's it to you?" *More than you realize!*

"Move." I said trying to fight back the tears. He looked puzzled and stepped aside and opened the door for me. I got in, struggled with the seat belt and zoomed off. He was standing there watching me, looking perplexed.

Chapter 12

Trust

I stormed upstairs to my bedroom as soon as I get home.

"Blair? Doll is that you?"

"Yeah!" I yelled.

"Are you okay? You look upset." Dad had walked upstairs to see me.

"Yes" I tried to say, but failed as I broke into a heavy sob. He pulled me in his arms and started to stroke my hair.

"Do you want to talk about it?"

"I don't know!" I whispered.

"Is it about the new kid at school?"

"Kind of."

"Connor?"

"Kind of."

"Do you know what it means to a dad when his daughter comes to him crying over two boys?" I looked up at him with my puffy red eyes.

"No, what?"

"It means it's time to bring out the shotgun!" I shoved him and started to laugh.

"It's stupid . . ." I wiped my eyes as I started to tell him the story of Connor finding me with Josh, I didn't tell him the part about Josh being my stalker; I know daddy would really bring out the shotgun then.

"Well Doll," he said after I had finished, "Connor will get over it and you will need to tell Josh what's really going on."

"What do you mean *what's really going on?*" He winked at me and told me to go talk to Connor.

"Thanks dad, I think I will go now, I'll be back in enough time to make dinner."

"Okay, I know it will all work out." He smiled to reassure me. "Don't worry about dinner I will figure out something."

"Thanks Daddy." I hugged him tightly and grabbed my bag and ran to my car. I stopped and took a deep breath before I turned the key. I looked in the mirror, and wiped my eyes, I was a mess! I started the car and backed out of the driveway.

There were a couple of times when I almost turned around to go back home, but I had to do this, I mean for goodness sake this kid is my best friend!

"Okay B, he will probably be mad that I'm even there, but just go at it easy and see what happens." I was talking to myself (another sign that I'm going crazy!)

"Ok I'll just be like 'hey what's up' . . ."

No that's too casual . . .

"Okay then I'll just plunge right into it; I'll be like 'I know you're mad, but just listen . . . .'"

Ohhhh, I don't know! Ugh!

When I pulled into Connor's driveway he was just getting out of his white mustang. He saw me and waited making it obvious that he was annoyed. I walked up to him and told him how sorry I was and if we could work it out . . . blah . . . blah . . . blah.

He was firm with a glare until he saw the first tear run down my cheek, he finally couldn't stand it anymore and grabbed me and hugged me. His big arms swallowed me.

"Con—can't . . . breath."

"Ha–ha I know!" he said, as he released his death grip, but not letting me go totally. "You know, I was going to see how long it took you to figure out that I forgave you already."

"What?"

"I've already forgiven you. I forgave you when I saw you pull up."

"But you looked so mad . . ." my voice was weak.

"Yeah, I just wanted you to feel bad for a little bit longer." He said with a wink, "And you're kind of cute when you're pleading." I laughed and blushed a little, I laughed even harder when he realized what he had said out loud.

"Don't think . . . I mean . . . gah!" I giggled,

"I understand bud, don't hurt yourself." This time I was the one to wink. "I knew you couldn't stay mad at me long." I teased.

"Don't push it!" he teased back. "So, how about that coffee?"

"Yeah, that sounds great." We caught up on the weeks we hadn't seen each other, as we rode in his mustang to the coffee shop. He talked about how he just got a job at a landscaping company, and how this crazy red headed freshman at school has been harassing him about being her boyfriend, you know the usual.

We laughed about how Jen has been trying to get us in the winter fashion show at school that she put together for a student council fund raiser, (she's really big in to the whole school spirit thing). After a while of making fun of Jen and the crazy redhead, it got quiet. I was looking out the window when I saw *Coco's* and I started thinking of Josh, Actually; getting scared all over again. I could feel my face getting hot with anger and my fingers starting to tremble; I felt my face twist trying to fight back tears.

"You okay?" he looked over to me. "Did I say something to make you mad?" I cleared my throat,

"No it's nothing . . . ." I stared out the window.

"It's Josh isn't it?"

"Uh, yeah, how did you know?"

"Jenna. Plus I saw the two of you at your car after school. Didn't seem like you guys were on good terms." He chuckled and smiled a huge grin.

"Ha, well you're right." We had arrived at the coffee shop and he got out and walked swiftly to open my door. He took my hand to help me out of his low seat and closed the door behind him.

"Do you want to talk about it?" he asked sincerely.

"Uh," I almost said 'no' but I got to thinking, after talking to Jen I needed him, and Connor always gives good advice. "Yeah actually I do, but only if you promise to keep it to yourself."

"Scouts honor." I rolled my eyes. We walked up to the counter and ordered our drinks.

"Um, I think I'll have a caramel frap," Connor said to the dark haired girl across the counter who had way too many face piercings.

"Ya think?" she said flatly.

"Uh? No, I know . . ."

"And what do you want?" she asked obviously bored out of her mind.

"I'll just have a caramel macchiato." She rolled her eyes and punched some buttons on the cash register. Connor paid the brat and we sat down by the window farthest from the front.

"Dang, what was her problem?" I said under my breath.

"Ha-ha I don't know, I bet it was her nose ring shoved to far up." I laughed.

"Okay, so tell me about Josh."

"Well okay, do you remember when I told you about the *fire drill* in eighth grade?"

"Yeah . . ."

"Well did I ever tell you that . . ." my voice faded, " . . . that I had a stalker?"

"Briefly"

"Yeah, well I just figured out . . . who it was."

"Whoa . . ." He looked deep in thought.

"But he doesn't know I'm me . . . ."

"I'm not following?"

"He doesn't know I'm the same Blair as the one in Florida." It took him a minute to get it,

"Oh!"

"Yeah and I chewed him out for hurting that poor girl." I laughed at myself for calling myself *that poor girl!* "I almost slipped and told him it was me. What should I do Connor? I don't want to tell him because he might start stalking me again." I paused and looked out the window, "I'm scared." I whispered so low I wasn't sure if he heard me. He blew out a long breath,

"Wow." He paused again, and surprised me by asking, "Are you sure you have Josh figured out?" I was shocked.

"What do you mean? I know Josh is a self-centered creep that gets a kick out of stalking girls who's had a hard time." I started to get hot with anger and confusion. "What are you trying to say?" He was now looking out the window.

"All I'm saying is make sure you have this right before you start jumping to conclusions." It hurt him to say that for some reason, I could see it written all over his face. *What! I'm not cutting to conclusions! I know for sure that Josh was the freak!*

"I thought you didn't like Josh?" I asked looking away, mad that he was on his side.

"Well . . . I don't," he smiled. "But that's only because he's stealing my best friend from me."

"Ok hold up! I'm confused so you aren't mad at him for doing that to me?"

"Of course I am, B," he paused, "I'm just trying to help you before you get even more hurt. Just go talk to him."

"**NO**! I can't! . . . He might start stalking me again."

"I will go with you if you want me to."

I pouted, "But why? Why tell him when he doesn't need to know?"

"He's going to figure it out sooner or later. Trust me it's going to be the best thing." We paused and stared at our coffee.

"Thank you, for everything," I finally said. I reached over the table and gave his hand a tight squeeze. "Don't worry about him stealing me You're my best friend." He looked out the window. "Well, it's getting late and I need to cook dinner for dad, because if he tries we will have our house in flames." we laughed and walked to the car.

"Hey you still up for the movie night tonight?" Connor asked.

"Oh yeah! I forgot! Do you mind running by the movie store?"

"No not at all. Should we pick up Jen? Remember the last time she found out that we picked the movie without her. Ha-ha she was so mad!"

"Oh yeah and she didn't talk to us for a week!" Jen is so funny when she's mad. She tries to act like nothing's wrong; she doesn't have a very good poker face.

"Yeah I guess so, let's get a pizza too."

I called my dad and told him we were picking up pizza for dinner and that they were coming over and then called Jen. When we pulled up she was already outside sitting on her porch steps. She waved and skipped to the door.

"Hey guys!" she smiled. "What kind of movie tonight? I was thinking romantic, either that or scary. Ya know I haven't seen a scary movie in a long time—" She kept rambling on and on. Connor looked at me and started laughing and rolled his eyes. I crossed mine, then he glared at me, this kept going on until Jen interrupted our back and forth.

"Are you guys like speaking in a silent language that I don't know about?" She nudged my arm and winked. I pulled down the sun visor and glared at her through the mirror. She stuck her tongue out at me, and winked again. Winking was her new "thing." Connor shifted in the driver's seat and acted like he hadn't seen or heard what Jen had said.

Con parked his pride and joy in our usual spot in front of the movie drop off slot, and then we went in to the newly built white and green building.

The bald fat man dressed in pleated khaki pants that were pulled up way past his big round Santa belly with suspenders and a navy polo that was supplied by the company, he was the manager of the store and he was working. We all shuddered. We've gotten kicked out of this store more than once for "being too loud." So we were careful to not let him see us. We stepped quickly behind a rack of old VHS's for sale. When the manager turned around we crouched and ran to the aisle of new releases.

We tried to keep quiet, but we just kept laughing, especially at Connor because every time one of us girls picked out a movie, he would crinkle his nose and make a remark that wasn't even funny, but we laughed at him anyway. We finally agreed on an old cheesy scary movie that none of us had heard of. We almost always pick an old movie; they seem to be the ones we all agree on. It's kind of our thing, pick dumb movies and then make fun of them after. We giggled in line as we tried to agree on what candy to get; this was always the hardest part. We all liked different things, but in the end we always get m&m's. Jen isn't crazy about them but she likes them okay.

When Bald Santa turned around and saw us standing there, he turned bright red! We held our breath so we wouldn't laugh, we managed to get out of there safely, Bald Santa, I think might have blown his top if there hadn't been other customers. As soon as we got out of the door we doubled over and busted out laughing.

"That was about the funniest thing I have ever seen!" Connor tried to catch his breath.

"I think B might choke!" Jen laughed even harder at me, as I sat on the curb hunched over shaking from laughing to hard. We stumbled to the car, and by the time we got to my house, we were in tears.

"Hey daddy!"

"Hello Mr. Chance." Connor echoed.

"What up Jay." Jen muttered as she made her way to the kitchen to set out the pizzas. He rolled his eyes at her and laughed, "Make yourselves at home."

The four of us played zilch, a dice game until after dark, and then we put in the movie. I sat in the middle of Jen and Connor on the big fluffy couch. Jen fell asleep with her head on my lap, as I stroked her soft hair, and her legs propped up on the arm of the couch. I ended up leaning against Connor with his arm on the back of the couch. Dad snored away in his big blue chair that no one was allowed to sit in. After the movie was over Conner gently patted my hand so I would wake up.

"Was I asleep?"

He smiled and chuckled, "yes all of you guys were out."

"Oh I'm sorry."

"It's not the first time." He winked.

"What time is it?" I whispered.

He leaned closer to me as he grabbed his phone out of his back pocket. "1:45"

"Dude."

"Yeah, well I better get Jen home. Text me tomorrow and let's do something." He whispered.

"Okay sounds good." I whispered back. He quietly got off the couch and gently picked Jen up and cradled her in his arms. She stirred but fell back asleep.

"Bye B." he whispered as I opened the door for him. "Thanks that was really fun."

"Yeah" I smiled and waved. I watched through the open door as he struggled to open the car door without waking up Jen. I skipped out into the moonlight and reached across Connor so I could open the door for him. He sat her down and buckled her in. I quietly closed the door with both hands to keep it from slamming and stepped back. He walked swiftly around the front of the car, as he did so it reminded me of earlier that day. When I found out Josh was my—my stalker.

Connor got in his car, turned over the engine and drove off.

"Bye Connor." I whispered to myself.

Dear mommy,

I'm exhausted; all these different emotions are wearing me out. But at the end of the day . . . I'm doing great! I just spent the night hanging with my two best friends. Just to chill and watch a movie and to not think about all that has been going on is awesome! I feel so blessed to have two people in my life that

Yvonne Didway

I can be totally me around. I can be Blair . . . the crazy, a little too nerdy at times, and always the just plain silly me. I wish you could have met them. You would love Jen, she reminds me of you. She is crazy funny and always knows how to make me laugh. Conner, well he is just Con . . . AMAZING! There is no better way to say it

Mammy, I love you and miss you . . . I need to get some sleep. Nightie Night!

Love your Bumble Bee :)

Chapter 13

Loud

She sat in a room that she used to know as comfort, solitude, refuge; now a locked dungeon closing in on her, claustrophobia was taking over, her head was spinning, her breaths short. She was drowning in a sea of lies, the waves crashing into her, does she open the door and let the angry mob tear her apart, or does she stay . . . . The splintering wood from the door is flying everywhere. She tries to run, but there's nowhere to go! With a loud crash the door falls to pieces, the mob runs in screaming. They start destroying everything in sight. They surround her and start swaying and chanting and spitting out insults—"How could you—how could you." She tries to scream but nothing comes out, she fights something inside her. Someone steps forward and slaps her across her face, she falls to the floor. Her arms are flailing in the air, her legs are kicking, and they pin her down to the ground, two on each arm and three on each leg. She screams "I'm sorry! I'm sorry!" They ignore her and keep her pinned. "I thought I was doing the right thing! Forgive me, I did not know what I had done!" they froze. Everything turned to darkness . . .

I screamed. I couldn't breathe. Everything was still dark. I couldn't sit up, I struggled to roll over to look at

81

the clock; it was only four a.m. Sweat was streaming from every inch of my body. "I don't understand." I whispered to myself. I was too exhausted to think. I quickly fell back into an uneasy sleep.

Chapter 14

Bruise

"Blaaaair, Blaaair." Dad said in a sing—songy voice as he rocked me so I would get up.

"Good morning, It's a bright Saturday morning," Dad said in his groggy morning voice. I rolled over to look at him through my squinted eyes. I saw him gasp.

"Honey, what did you do?"

"What? What's wrong?" I asked in a sleepy voice.

"Did you get in a fight or something?"

"What?" my voice broke.

"Doll, go look at your face!" He demanded.

I fell out of bed (I'm not very coordinated in the morning) and dragged myself to the bathroom trying to figure out what he was talking about and why my head was spinning. I felt like I was walking on the ceiling, the hall mirror was distorted and the hall its self was going in circles. When I looked up to see myself in the mirror, I gasped my head felt woozy. The green eyed person that stared back at me had dark circles around her eyes and a faint blue bruise on her upper left cheek, a small cut above her right brow and a busted lower lip. I gasped. Everything was spinning; my head was throbbing so hard I could feel it through my whole body. I felt myself start to fall, and then everything was black.

"Blair!" Nothing happened.

"Blair! Wake up!"

★   ★   ★

Beep . . . beep . . . beep . . . "She okay . . . beep . . . fainted . . . beep . . . head . . . . trauma . . . needs . . . beep . . . sleep . . ." is all I heard before I fell back to sleep.

★   ★   ★

When I woke up, who knows when, I could hear voices murmuring in the background, I tried to open my eyes, but they were swollen shut. I lifted my hands to wipe my eyes, but they were tied down. I tried to wiggle out of whatever was holding me down, but it was too tight. I was brought back to my dream where the mob had her pinned to the ground so she couldn't move. I started to scream, I was living my dream! I heard a high pitched voice yell for help—Another deeper one yelling to untie me, I felt someone with cold hands touch my arm and say-

"It's okay Blair, it's Dr. Kin, you are okay."

"UNTIE ME!" I screamed.

"I can't do that just yet, you will hurt yourself. Now calm down, you are okay," said the old gentle voice.

I screamed again "Why can't I see?" I felt a gentle cold hand wipe my eyes. I tried again to open them, but I still couldn't see. "PLEASE! I'm begging you! Why can't I see?" I sobbed.

84

"Blair, calm down and I will make you see again," said the doctor. After a few more people telling me that I was okay and to calm down, I finally got exhausted and stopped my tantrum. My head was still pounding, but not nearly as badly as the last time I woke up. The doctor put a cold ice pack on my eyes and wiped them again and administered some kind of drops that stung; naturally my eyes reacted to the drops and I started to cry. I felt the hot tears run down my face and drip off of my chin to my chest. I could only open them part of the way because they were still swollen. I saw a nurse reading some kind of chart, my dad sitting on the side with his head down, his hands were rubbing his temples and the Doc was staring at me. The room was white, too white. It smelled like powdered latex gloves and some kind of sweet medicine. There was a monitor beside me that was beeping. I looked down and saw an IV In my arm, *ugh I hate needles.*

"Can you please untie me now?" I asked quietly, and as sweetly as possible.

"If you promise not to go crazy on me." The doc chuckled and tore the Velcro straps off one at a time.

"I'm sorry; I thought I was somewhere else," I said to the doc.

"I know, that's why you were strapped down," the doc said with a smile as he left the white room.

"Hey dad . . . I am so sorry, I didn't mean—" Dad cut me off, "It's okay, doll, you couldn't help it."

"See, that's where you're wrong. I could have helped it!" I yelled as I jerked my head down.

"I should have known. Why did you tell me it was a random dream?"

"I-I thought it would pass. I didn't want you to worry—I'm so sorry!"

"What did you dream about last night?" Dad asked trying to put the puzzle pieces together. I stopped and thought for a moment.

"The same dreams I dream every night. The ones that started after the *letters.*" I shivered at the thought.

"Was anything different?" Dad asked. I tried to think the whole night over again. "Ye-yes" every bone in my body was shaking.

"What happened different?"

"I-I-I—saw them-"

"Who did you see?"

"Th-the mob-they ca-came in!"

"Where? Where did they come in?"

"THE GIRL'S ROOM!" I broke into a heavy sob covering my face with my taped up hands. My head started spinning again from the heavy sobs.

"It's okay; it's going to be okay. I'm sorry I didn't mean to upset you. I'm going to call the psychiatrist."

★   ★   ★

I was at the hospital for the rest of that day; I just had a few bruises on my arms and face and a slight concussion. The Doc said that when I was dreaming about the "mob" hurting the girl, I was trying to fight them off of her, therefore I was hitting myself. The confusing part about that is why would I hit myself when I was trying to fight the mob off?

When we left the hospital we went straight to the psychiatrist, where I told her about all the letters I got, and how at first they were just annoying pranks, then they changed to outright mean, and about my stalker. I told her that they scared me so much that I refused to go to school. I would have dreams of me stuck in the hallways with some random person's shadow following me around, but then they changed into a girl, I never saw her face. She would be trapped in a room or in the middle of a street with people about to stone her.

Every night was a different dream. It was always the same girl and the same blurred faces of the mob. I would wake up screaming, my dad finally got so concerned that he took me to see a psychiatrist. She helped a tremendous amount, but not enough to keep me going to school, that's when my dad said it was time to move. The dreams stopped shortly after I left Florida two years ago, but with Josh moving here, I guess that brought them back. This was the first time I actually saw the "mob" come in to the girl's room, I couldn't make out their faces, but I could tell they all looked alike.

After we got home from going to the shrink's I went straight to bed, I was so exhausted, and I slept a dreamless sleep.

★   ★   ★

A couple days later on Monday at school, Jenna about had a fit over my bruises,

"OMG girl what did you do?" Jenna looked at me horrified.

"I fell off my bike." I looked away so she didn't know I was lying.

"Why were you riding your bike when you have a car?"

"Um to get some exercise, you know to get out."

"Wow you're weird." We laughed and walked in to find Connor laughing with some of his guy friends by the water fountain.

"Whoa, dude, what happened, get in a fight?" Connor said.

"Can you seriously see me getting in a fight?" I said pointing to my face.

"Ha, ha I like the new look, it makes you look. Tough, you know, like it says 'don't mess with me or I'll kick your butt'."

"You are a freak." I said teasing him.

"Ha, ha shut up." For the rest of the day people kept asking me what happened and I think I told the bike story like fifty times.

I saw Josh and about broke down but I got a hold of myself.

After school, I went to Connor's to do some homework and we ended up talking about the Josh situation.

"Have you talked to Josh yet?"

"Umm, that would be a negative." I pointed to my face again.

"Well, you should."

"I still don't understand why I need to tell him that it's me."

"Because . . . You just do, okay?"

"Oh my goodness just tell me, I know you know something, so just tell me!"

He paused "I can't."

He looked away. I stared at him with disgust for a whole three seconds till finally I said, "Why? I mean I deserve to know, this is about me you know?"

"Look Blair, you are right, this is about you, but it's also about Josh. You need to get this straightened out—Fast." I started to get upset. "I'm sorry, I know this is hard, but you need to do this."

"I just don't understand—Why him? Why me? Why now? You don't understand—he freaking stalked me! Do you not know what happens to some of the girls that get stalked?"

"Yes, I know what happens, but I don't think this is like that. If it was, wouldn't he have already done something?"

"I don't know!" I covered my face, wincing in the process from the pain.

"Blair. Look at me." He lifted my chin with his pointer finger and looked deep into my tear reddened eyes.

"If I knew you were going to get hurt I wouldn't tell you to go talk to him. Now, are you sure it was him?" I moved my chin from under his finger.

"Ninety nine percent sure . . . He has the exact same email address, and when you think about it, it does sort of add up."

"Okay, well that's a start but how do you know it wasn't one of his friends trying to scare you?"

"How do *you* know it wasn't him trying to scare me?"

"Okay, you got me there. What if your dad was right, what if they really were genuine apologies?"

"I would believe that if they were all nice, but they went from straight hateful to uber nice. Plus there wasn't just one or two, it was like twenty or thirty . . . that's just going overboard."

"True—what kind of things would they say?"

"Things like 'Nice display double A!' or 'You pretty much win the weirdest, flattest, most awkward girl award.' Then later his big thing was 'forgive them for they know not what they do." I shuddered.

"Okay, yeah, the first one was just mean and scary, but what if he felt sorry and decided to go another route?"

"I don't know. I thought about that, but why would a big headed skater boy feel sorry for an invisible girl?"

"Maybe, because he was invisible too." I stared at him like he was crazy.

"Are you kidding me right now? You can't be serious. Josh invisible?" I started to laugh, that was about the funniest thing I'd heard in a long time. He ignored me and went back to reading.

When I got home that night from Connor's, I went straight to the box of letters from the stalker, I put them in order from the first one to the last. I stapled them to my huge cork board, so I could shove it under my bed when I was finished.

Dear mommy,

I'm sorry, I hurt myself again. I don't understand what brings this on and why it won't go away. I want to forget it all and move on. I want to be a new person and to be free from this turmoil. I thought I had done that but now this, how did I let it get so bad . . . I was so happy; I had a new life, new friends and a new me . . . I promised myself not to let this ever bother me again; it was over, in the past, that was the old Blair. I promised that I wouldn't let myself think about it anymore, but my mind is refusing to let it go, I never stopped having those dreams, yes I moved on into my new life, but my old life never really went away. It has always been in the back of my mind. It's all a mess mommy.

I love you mama</3

Your little broken bee.

Chapter 15

Rush

When I walked up to school the next morning, I saw Josh sitting by the fountain again. I tried to get past him, but he ran after me. I tried to go around him, but he kept cutting me off. I started shaking. When I got close to the door he ran and jumped in front of me and opened the door and waited for me to walk through. I gave him a scared/confused look with my bruised face and walked in. I walked right into a crowd of people talking so he couldn't see where I was going. Once I got out of the mess of students, I ran straight for Connor's first class.

I didn't stop running until I got to the classroom. I skidded to a stop at the door frame and hunched over trying to catch my breath. Connor rushed over to me.

"Are you okay?" Connor asked alarmed.

"Uh? Yeah . . ." I took a deep breath, "just out . . . of breath."

"Did you run all the way here?"

"Yup."

He chuckled and asked, "And why did you run all the way here?"

"I didn't run all the way here from my house, just from the front door of the school." He laughed at me again.

"Wow, B, that's a long way!" he said sarcastically.

"Oh shut up!"

"Ha, ha, so are you going tell me why you ran to see me? I mean I know I'm cute but you didn't have to run." I shoved him and rolled my eyes.

"Josh was acting really weird. He kept cutting me off so I couldn't walk away from him. He opened the door for me and followed me inside." He gave me a look that said 'and?'"

"He was probably just trying to be nice."

"I don't know why I come to you when you're clearly no help!"

"Sorry. I'm a guy—ha but, hey, will you help me with homework again today?"

"Sure, but only if you walk me to class."

"I was going to do that anyway, but sure." I smiled at him and we walked out of the classroom, "I don't want to go alone. So I meant to tell you the other day, but I got distracted—" I pointed to my lovely eye. "thanks for taking Jen home Friday, that was really sweet of you."

"Oh yeah, it was no problem until she woke craving a big mac from McDonalds, but of course she didn't want to go to the one over by 5th street 'it's gross' she said, so she demanded that I take her to the one downtown that's like 20 minutes away."

"Ha-ha that stinks, did she super size it and get fries?" I giggled.

"Actually she did! I swear that girl could out eat Logan before a big game."

"Seriously I know, my dad literally has to hide his hoho's and dr. peppers under the kitchen sink just to keep Jen, the human garbage disposal, from consuming them."

"Ha-ha you would think after eleven years you would get used to seeing someone eat as much and Michael Phelps but somehow it never ceases to amaze me."

"I don't understand how that girl stays so small . . . has it really been eleven years that you guys have known each other?"

"Yes unfortunately." he winked. "Ever since that time in kindergarten when Betty big booty," he started to chuckle, it took him a minute to catch his breath. "Sorry, never can seem to control myself from calling her that. But anyways, ever since I saw Betty sitting on Jen in the sandbox claiming she stole her shovel. Jen looked like a squished spider all her limbs sprawled out and kicking, what kid wouldn't run to her rescue? It took me and two other boys to get Betty off of her. Once we finally pried big Betty off, Jen gasped for air and clung to me, thanking me. I've never let her out of my sight since. I thought you had heard that story before?"

"I have, but I just still can't believe that was eleven years ago, and plus it makes me laugh every time I hear it." I giggled to myself as I walked into class.

"Connor you really are such a great friend."

"Where did that come from?"

"I don't know, you just are, and I thought you should know."

I spent the rest of the day going from class to class, ignoring the continual stares at my battered face, and the whispers from behind, rumors have already started, but I could honestly care less. I've got all the friends I need, and around here people live off of drama. This will pass in an hour once they find a new victim to feed off of. In bio Jen and I made plans to go shopping, get a mani-pedi, and do avocado masks, it's our back to school girls weekend (for the third time this year).

Jen was messing around on her blackberry when she looked up all bright eyed. "There's this huge sale going on at Coach that we need to hit up also." She whispered beside me.

"Ha-ha okay, we can do that."

"Do you still want to have movie night with Con Friday?"

"Yeah, maybe we can convince him to do avocado masks with us." She threw her manicured hand up,

"Girl, he probably would too." I laughed and went back to my book.

After school I called my dad to tell him I was going to Connor's, so not to expect me home till later. The first couple of days of school he likes to take me to and from school so we can spend time together because he works all the time at the hospital, but after about a week, I just end up driving myself to school. I found Connor leaning against his car waiting for me, texting someone.

"So you do know how to text?" I asked as I waited for him to unlock the door. He just glared at me. "How has your day been?"

"Eh, it was school. You?"

"Same. Is Jen coming?"

"Nah, she had to go work at the beauty shop with her mom." We got in the car; I reached over to put my seat belt on and glanced in the back seat to find Josh sitting there smirking . . .

Chapter 16

~~Trust~~

"I can't believe this!" I yelled as I stumbled out of the car.

"Blair, come back. Trust me, just get in the car!" Connor chased after me. I looked at him through teary eyes.

"How could you?"

"Blair, look I know you're mad at me but please—" I cut him off.

"Trust you? Is that what you were going to say?"

"Well, yeah, but please just give it a try. I'll be there the whole time." My guard came down and the real emotions flowed.

"I-I-I can't." I looked away. He grabbed me by the shoulders and brought me into a hug.

"It's going to be ok." he said while smoothing my hair.

"You promise?"

"Promise."

"Fine." I whispered. We walked back to the car and he opened the door and helped me in.

"Um, do I need to go?" Josh asked.

"Yes." I muttered under my breath. Connor glared at me.

"No you're fine, she's just a little upset about something." He gave me a nudge and a glare.

★   ★   ★

Once we got to the house, I excused myself to the bathroom to clean up from my fit. The boys started on their homework and Connor acted like everything was just peachy.

As I walked out of the bathroom, I heard voices talking in a whisper.

"She . . . okay?" I think, Josh said.

"Yeah . . . she'll . . . fine."

"Why . . . do . . . I . . . need . . . to . . . here?"

"Needs . . . tell . . ." That's when I walked in and said "hey."

"Hey, feeling better?" Connor asked jokingly.

"Oodles." I said sarcastically. "So w-what are we working on?" I asked shyly.

"History paper . . . ugh," Connor said.

"So, what was with Mrs. Webs today? Man was she . . . rarer." Josh made a gesture like a tiger. Connor thought that was the funniest thing since standup comedy, I just faked a giggle.

"Hey, Blair, can you help me in the kitchen with the drinks?" Connor asked while kicking me under the table.

"Sure?" Connor walked me to the kitchen, and talked small talk to make it not that obvious that he was trying to get away from Josh. Once we got far enough the mood got serious.

"He doesn't seem to know it's you." Connor whispered.

"No dip, Sherlock." I said while crossing my eyes. "Isn't that why I'm here? Ya know, to tell him it's me?"

"Well, yeah, but I didn't know if he was suspicious or not."

"Okay, whatever, how do you want me to bring it up?"

"Ask him about his old school . . . I don't know, figure it out!" he whispered.

"You're the one that wants me to do this, not me remember!" I whispered harshly back.

"Yeah, yeah, whatever, but you can do it, I know you can." He gave me reassuring wink and grabbed some sodas from the fridge and walked back in to the living room.

"Whoa, where did he go?" Connor asked.

"Umm, maybe to the bathroom." I guessed. We set the drinks down on the table, and saw a note.

Hey sorry for the urgent leave, my dad called,
and said I had to go.
Josh

We stood there a moment looking at the note.

"I hope everything is okay," Connor finally said, as he looked at me with concern in his eyes.

"I personally think it's weird . . . but, whatever." I paused, "Wait how did he leave without a car?" Connor paused and then ran to the door to see if Josh took his car.

"My car is still here. I bet his dad came and picked him up."

"But we were only in the kitchen for like, a minute that was a really fast pick up."

"Yeah . . ."

★   ★   ★

We found out later that day that his dad did pick him up and they went straight home. We don't know why he had to go so fast. Connor dropped me off at my house later that day. I went to my room and drug out the corkboard. As I scanned over it I could see a pattern forming: emails, text, and then the letters. The first few emails and such were blonde jokes and teasing about double A. Then they started to get really mean, hateful even. Then sincere, they still were jokes but they were heavier. I didn't get to finish because my dad knocked on the door telling me someone was here to see me. I walked down the stairs and saw Josh sitting on the big leather couch. He stood.

"Uh, hey." he looked nervous.

"Hi?" I gave him a weird look, and then looked around to make sure my dad was near. "Why are you here?"

He chuckled nervously. "Umm, I'm not sure actually, I guess because I wanted to see you."

I watched him carefully. "Sorry, but I'm not following?"

"I don't know how to say this . . . the reason I left early today from Connor's was because . . ." he paused to think, "because when I saw you crying I got this really weird flash back . . ." he paused again, "It was of that girl I told you about." I started to shake. He continued looking down, "After the fire drill, I barely saw her, when I did see her, she looked . . . scared or even sometimes like *she* had been crying." I started to tremble even more as he was talking. As he told his story, I kept having flashbacks of the days I was at school-

★　　★　　★

"Daddy please!" my small voice pleaded.

"Doll, you need to try to go, if you get scared I will be there as fast as I can."

"But Daddy, I'm scared now!"

"I know doll. I will be close. I told your principal what's going on and he said he would keep a close eye on you and, if anything happens, he will call me right away."

★　　★　　★

"Blair, are you okay?" I was brought back to reality.

"W-w-what?"

"You're shaking?"

"Oh, yeah I–I'm fine." I nodded to reassure him. "Just got a little distracted. What were you saying?"

"I was telling you about the girl at my old school."

"Oh, yeah."

"Okay, so like I said before she didn't come to school very often, and when she did she looked scared. I tried to find out if she had some kind of disability or if something happened to her."

An image of me sitting alone in the cafeteria trembling flashed before my eyes.

He continued, "I started to feel bad for her, after the fire drill her friends deserted her, they didn't want to be seen with double A."

★　　★　　★

"Hey Blair" someone whispered behind me. I spun around to find Trish from Beta club.

"Oh hey!" I said shocked that she wanted to talk to me.

"Shh keep it down!" she whispered again.

"Why? We are in the bathroom?"

"Uh . . . I just don't want to be heard, okay?"

"Okay fine . . . . Whatcha need?"

"Umm . . . my mom said I can't go to your house today . . . I have to . . . uh garden . . . I have to garden with my grandma . . ." she looked away from me. I looked down, I was figuring it out, it wasn't that her mom was making her; it was because she didn't want to.

"Oh, okay . . . I understand." I walked out of the bathroom, hurt, leaving Trish behind.

★　　★　　★

"-the few friends she had were whittling down." Josh kept talking in a slow steady pace. "I just don't understand . . ." he shook his head rapidly. "I know the fire drill was embarrassing but why would she look so scared?"

"JUST STOP! PLEASE! STOP!" I yelled as I ran up to my room. I couldn't take it anymore. I heard footsteps behind me.

"Blair, wait! What's going on?"

"Stop. Please. Stop." I said through tears. I was hunched over my corkboard crying, the tears spilling onto the crumpled pages. Josh gently came to sit beside me on the floor. He started to stroke my back, but I jerked away.

"JUST LEAVE ME ALONE! YOU'VE DONE ENOUGH DAMAGE!"

"Blair what are you talking about?"

"IT'S ME! CANT YOU SEE ITS ME? I'M THE GIRL YOU TORTURED!" I paused to breathe, "I know what you're doing. How could someone be so sick? Why are you doing this to me?" I whispered through tears.

"I'm sorry but I don't know what you are talking about?"

"LOOK! RIGHT HERE, JUST LOOK AT WHAT YOU DID!" I jabbed my finger toward the corkboard sitting on the floor. He looked at where I was pointing; he paused, noticing for the first time what I was bending over. After a long blank stare, he sat down on my bed and put his head in his hands.

"I'm sorry." is all he said.

"Get out." I tried to say calmly. He didn't move. "Get. Out. Now." He stumbled to his feet and looked at me through wet red eyes.

"Please, let me explain, we were young and stupid . . . . Please."

"Out." I pointed to the door.

Chapter 17

Scared

Dear mommy,

I was lonely and scared. Where else was I supposed to go? The only place I feel comfort. When I sit on this grassy hill, I feel powerful, like I could be anything. It's a good place to sit and think or even to cry when you don't know what to think. I don't have a name for this place; it's just a place to go when I don't know where to go. I am so confused. Why would Josh be so concerned about me, the other me? He said it himself, "We were young and stupid." So, obviously it was him, and possibly his basketball buddies. But why, after doing so much damage and have so much time pass would he start to feel sorry for her-me now? I know three things for a fact: one he was my stalker. Two, he feels bad about it, and three, many people will be forever changed because of the ever so innocent fire drill.

-Your little bumble bee <3

After staying awhile at my spot it started getting dark so I collected my things and went home.

⋆　　⋆　　⋆

Shaking, terrified begging for them to stop. She was thrown in the middle of an angry mob, screaming at her, arms ready with their stones. She was tangled in a web of lies, tangled so tightly she twisted and fought to get out. She waited for the first accuser to throw a heavy sharp rock. She trembled on the ground, guilt from her once a little white lie kept taunting her to give up. She tried to stand to run, but the mob pushed her back to the ground she fell to the middle. She heard an angry deep voice yell, "Throw on three. One, Two, Three-

"WAIT!" The girl screamed! "Please just let me explain!"

"NO," yelled an angry voice. "You've done enough damage! Throw!" the girl screamed again. She covered her head as the stones pelted her again and again.

"STOP! PLEASE STOP!" The image faded into darkness.

I sat up straight. I brushed back my hair that was stuck to my face with my small cold hand. *What's going on . . . ? I don't get this?* I started to shake I was so scared.

Chapter 18

Answers

Dear Blair,

Please take the time to read this. I know you are upset about what happened in eighth grade, but please understand that was in the past and I was a stupid arrogant kid. I can't explain why the fire drill happened, because I do not know.

The emails and texts and some of the other things you got were from me and a few of the boys on the basketball team. We created an email account just for that, skaterfreak21. I was in the gym when the fire drill happened and, I'm not going to lie or deny it, I thought it was funny at the time. Looking back on it, I think it was a very harsh and stupid thing for someone to do. We started the emails that same day; we thought it would be funny to egg it on. I didn't know the boys were going to go as far as sneaking to your house at night to see what information they could gather for the next email or text. I was not a part of that. After the first few emails, I started to get bored with it so I stopped being a part of the crew.

About two and a half months after the fire drill, I noticed that you didn't come to school very often. I asked the boys if I could see what all they had sent to you. They showed me and I was horrified. I tried to see if you were okay but something would always get in the way. So, I threatened them that if they didn't stop, I was going to do something about it. About a week or so after, they decided they had done enough. I however, took that opportunity to change the letters to apology letters. I wasn't thinking about how you would take it. I didn't realize until I was at your house yesterday looking at the letters that they seemed more like I was mocking or even sketchy about it.

My purpose was not to scare you but to simply say "I'm sorry." After I wrote the first one I thought it would be all good, but I didn't see you the next day, so I wrote another one, and so forth. I will admit I did watch you; I was concerned that the boys and maybe even I had scared you or over did it. I watched you mostly at school, and occasionally would walk by your house to see if you were home. I can promise you that it wasn't meant out of harm, it just kind of formed into a habit to look out for you. When I didn't see you at school for a few weeks, I got worried and went to your house to see if you were okay, but I found it empty. My heart broke because I knew I had a part in your leaving . . .

I am truly sorry for my part in all this, can you ever forgive me? I didn't know what I was doing, things got way out of hand. I hope to talk this out with you in person someday.

Sorry,
Josh

Chapter 19

Skeptical

I began to realize it on the Hill. The Hill opened my eyes to another world. My world. It's crazy how one simple hill can change a life. My life.

As I sat and re-read Josh's letter the next day at my spot on the hill, I couldn't help but cry. It was such a relief to know the truth. But I was still skeptical. I tried to take deep breaths and lay down just to clear my mind.

I couldn't get any of this mess out of my head; I was still so confused on so many things. Dreams, the girl in the dreams,

"Oh come on, please help me." I yelled to the sky.

The word grace popped in my head.

Grace . . . what about grace?

The note.

Josh's note . . . forgive Josh even though he doesn't deserve it . . .

I was sitting in my normal Indian style position staring at the scattered little buildings and trees that lie deep down in the valley, struggling and thinking about what I should do next. I leaned my head back so that the newly awakened sun could dry my tears.

★　　★　　★

I heard footsteps crunching on rocks behind me. Josh stopped when I turned around.

He looked nervous, skeptical probably expecting me to jump up and slap him across the face.

"How did you find me?" I asked.

"I talked to Connor, and he told me where I could probably find you." I patted to dewy ground beside me, signaling him to sit down. He hesitated, but finally agreed to sit. He leaned back and stretched his long legs out, one over the other.

"Look," I said trying not to sound skittish, "I'm not sure how to take all this, I spent so much time thinking one thing, feeling one thing, and now that all of that has changed . . . I don't know what to think or feel . . ." I paused and ran my hands over the grass. "-but whatever really happened, the reasons for all that mess, I just want you to know that . . . that I've decided . . . I'm going to forgive you." Josh looked up surprised.

"I-I-I wasn't sure how you'd take this." He said nervously, "I have thought over all of your possible reactions, but you have surprised me, I didn't think you would handle it like you have." It was silent as we absorbed the breathtaking view.

"Why . . . . why did all this happen?" I said ruining the moment.

"I-I don't know, I wish I did, I really have no idea." he paused, "I'm so sorry." He glanced away with a pained look on his face.

"Me too, but through all of that I grew up . . ." It was quiet. "Do you have any ideas why the fire drill happened?" He paused, and sucked in a deep breath.

"I don't know . . . I've been thinking about it a lot and . . ." he stopped for a moment and then continued, "The only thing I can come up with is that it might have had something to do with Taylor–" *That would make sense of her glaring at me in the hallway. I just thought that maybe she thought of herself as too good for me.* "You see, when I first saw you in the hallway, I noticed that you looked so timid." he chuckled. "There was something inside of me that pulled me toward you. At first I just thought you were cute," he blushed, which surprised me, because a guy like him doesn't blush. "I thought I could get anything I wanted, so I tried to flirt with you. But after I realized how shy you were, it just pushed me toward you even more. I actually started to care for you, instead of it just being a challenge to me or something. I have a theory;" He sat up straight and leaned towards me. "I think Taylor noticed my attention toward you and she got jealous. That's why she planned the fire-drill." I glanced at him with a confused expression.

"So, let me get this straight, you think Taylor was jealous of me, because you were just being nice?"

He chuckled, "Well, yeah, and maybe a little flirty, you have to remember she was my girlfriend at the time and she was the jealous type." He laughed nervously.

"Oh." We sat in silence for what seemed like a lifetime; suddenly, I burst out in laughter. He turned to face me with a humorous expression.

"What's so funny?" he asked. It took me a minute to catch my breath.

"It's funny how one moment can change something so drastically, like a life . . . even when it's as ridiculous as some girl getting jealous of another girl over a stupid boy–no offense."

"None taken."

"This was blown way out of proportion!" We laughed hysterically.

"Yeah, it really was."

Chapter 20

Broken

As I walked down the deserted downtown streets, I took in the sight of broken windows, spray painted doors, turned over cars-it hurt to look at it all. I came to a little yellow house, something pulled me toward it. I opened the squeaky door, and heard shouting upstairs. I ran up the stairs and covered my ears; the screams of the people were so loud and awful! I ran back down and out the door. I walked around the house and saw the window that led inside the room where the mob was trying to break into. I climbed up the overgrown vines. I got to the awning and crouched down so I could look through the window.

It was my room, light blue paint on the walls, my unmade bed in the middle with a nightstand beside it facing the closet door. What's going on? I noticed someone hunched over on the colorful bed. Matted dark blonde hair pressed against her neck. She was using her small pale hands to cover her face. She was trembling. She looked up with her tear stained face and started to shake even more. The door was giving way, she jumped off the bed and tried to run but there was nowhere to go! She pressed herself against the wall wrinkling a poster. The door gave in! She started to scream; the mob rushed in and grabbed her! I started to scream and bang on the window! I knew the people in the mob! It was the boys from the basketball team and Josh. There were more and they kept rushing in like a floodgate finally breaking free. It seemed like hundreds! They all looked the same. I didn't know who they were at first until one decided to face the window. It was another me, tens and tens of Blair's! I couldn't move I studied the face that looked at me, small pale with crazy green eyes that had a hint of sadness. I looked past her, (me) and saw that the other part of the mob was carrying her down the stairs. The 'me' that was staring at me realized that they were leaving and ran to catch up with them. I was stunned. I finally snapped out of my haze. I climbed down the thick vines, scratching me in my haste. I ran to see where they were going to take her. As I came to where they were at the end of the street, I noticed that there was a red circle painted on the ground; there were rocks all inside that were stained red. They threw her to the middle.

"Stop! Please stop!" I yelled! They didn't hear me. I pushed through the thick crowd making my way closer. I started to cry. The girl in the middle who was in my room was another me! What's going on? I ran to the middle of the red circle shielding the broken me; I screamed again, "stop! Please stop!" They froze and stopped their screaming and looked at me. "Listen, stop she didn't know what was going on! You don't need to hurt her anymore. I bent down and helped the frail girl up. Well, me, up. As we stood up together, clutching to each other, the mob drifted off one by one, until it was just me and . . . me.

I woke up for the first time not scared. I was crying, though, but soon the tears turned into tears of joy. I was so relieved to know why I was having all of those dreams. I realized that I had been beating myself up for the past three years. All I had to do was tell myself the truth. I hope now that if I dream, they will be about my new life. My refreshed life, the one without lies or confusion. I feel like a new person. All it took was the truth to make me whole again!

★   ★   ★

A week later after I talked to Josh, I went back to the same place, not to think but just to clear my head. As I sat in my Indian style position taking in the view, I heard footsteps behind me. I turned around and found Connor approaching. He came over and sat next to me.

"You know how I knew Josh wasn't going to hurt you?" I stayed silent waiting for him explain.

"I knew everything. Josh called me the day I saw you at the coffee shop with him, he tried to explain what happened, and somehow he ended up telling me that you reminded him of a girl he knew in eighth grade who was actually named Blair too. I don't know how, but I figured it out. I knew he was the guy that followed you, but to be honest, even as much as I didn't like the guy, I knew he wasn't a bad guy. I put his pieces and yours of the story together. I knew the truth, but, I knew you needed to find it out yourself.

I fell silent. I could feel all the stress from the past events melting off of me. I don't remember why or how it happened exactly, but somehow I ended up kissing him. It was a really awkward moment . . . I pulled away and nervously giggled trying to hide the blush making its way to my cheeks. The blush won.

"What in the world was that about?" He laughed.

"I'm sorry . . ." I blushed again, this time surrendering to the blood rushing to my face. I glanced over and caught him staring at me with a serious expression on his face. I bowed my head trying to decipher what just happened and why I just did that . . . Seconds later, I felt a warm hand gently pull my chin up, so he could look me in the eyes. He whispered with a smile, "I forgive you." Before I knew it, my breath was taken away by a tender pressure that rested against my lips.

I realized that I've been saying the whole time that the hill changed my life, but that's not true . . . even the incident is just what happened . . . the hill is just where I figured it all out. What changed my life were two simple words: Grace and truth.

Epilogue

Dear mommy,

I learned that the smallest things can change lives. If it wasn't for the fire drill and the pressure it put on me to grow up in some areas, I would still be the same sad, quiet Blair. I wish It didn't happen like it did, but it's the past and some things are meant to be cherished and others to be forgotten. Parts of this story will be left behind, and that's fine with me, but there are parts that I don't want to forget, parts that really did change my life, for the good. I had to go back and face the cold hard past to be able to move forward.

-your little bumble bee <3